D0115580

BLACK
LIGHT

BLACK
LIGHT

STORIES

KIMBERLY
KING
PARSONS

VINTAGE BOOKS
A DIVISION OF PENGUIN RANDOM HOUSE LLC
NEW YORK

A VINTAGE BOOKS ORIGINAL, AUGUST 2019

Copyright © 2019 by Kimberly King Parsons

All rights reserved. Published in the United States by Vintage Books, a division of Penguin Random House LLC, New York, and distributed in Canada by Penguin Random House Canada Limited, Toronto.

Vintage and colophon are registered trademarks of Penguin Random House LLC.

This is a work of fiction. Names, characters, places, and incidents either are the product of the author's imagination or are used fictitiously. Any resemblance to actual persons, living or dead, events, or locales is entirely coincidental.

Several of the stories first appeared, in slightly different form, in the following publications: "The Animal Part" in *Gigantic,* No. 4 (2012); "Black Light" as "Fellowship" in *Black Warrior Review* (2016); "Fiddlebacks" in *New South* (2016); "In Our Circle" in *NANO Fiction* 10, No. 1 (Fall 2016); "Into the Fold" in *The Fiddleback* 2, No. 4; "The Light Will Pour In" in *Ninth Letter* (Fall/Winter 2017–2018); "Guts" as "Nothing Before Something" in *Indiana Review* (Winter 2017); "The Soft No" in *Joyland* (2017); "We Don't Come Natural to It" in *No Tokens,* No. 6 (Spring/Summer 2017).

The Cataloging-in-Publication Data is on file at the Library of Congress.

Vintage Books Trade Paperback ISBN: 978-0-525-56350-1
eBook ISBN: 978-0-525-56351-8

Book design by Elizabeth A. D. Eno

www.vintagebooks.com

Printed in the United States of America
10 9 8 7 6 5 4 3 2 1

For Ronnie

Cut me open and the light streams out.
—Richard Siken, *Crush*

CONTENTS

BLACK
LIGHT

GUTS

WHEN I START DATING TIM, an almost-doctor, all the sick, broken people in the world begin to glow. Light pours from careful limpers in the streets, from the wheezers and wet coughers who stop right in front of me to twist out their lungs. People I once found gross or contagious are radiant, gleaming with need. The newborn on my bus shines like swaddled halogen—harnessed to his tired mother's chest, he turns his jaundiced little face toward me, no matter where I sit. I've always been a noticer, but this tug from the hearts and minds and ailing bodies of strangers—this is all Tim's fault.

"How can you stand it?" I say to him.

We're at the movies, in the very back row, the theater—

I swear—full of hidden rashes and shriveled limbs. I tell Tim that even the Jesus screamer—the guy who paws through my garbage and sometimes shits on my front stoop—he is now incandescent, his eyes drippy with hope.

"It's too much," I say. "Beautiful, shattered people everywhere. Is this what it's like to be you?"

We're too early, as usual. Trivia and local business ads flash on the big screen. The movie Tim has chosen is a comedy, a mistaken-identity caper with a pug dog in a supporting role.

"Nah," Tim says, and yawns. One of his eyes closes. "I turn it on and off."

Tim is a week into his internal medicine rotation, and I have so many questions. I'd rather be sitting across from him at the Chinese place, dumplings on the way, listening to him talk about patient histories and lab data, about how best to deliver bad news. I want to absorb it all—the lining of every wrinkle in his brain. But Tim is too tired to eat, exhausted from being on call. He picks movie dates because when the house bulbs dim he can drift off. He thinks he's got me fooled.

"They're all so fragile," I say. I mean the strange heads in front of us, other people waiting for the lights to go out.

"Well, yeah," Tim says. His device vibrates in his pocket. He takes it out and taps on it. "But unless I'm looking at somebody's chart I don't really think of them that way."

Tim's device flashes. He taps and taps. "Goddamn it," he says. "Give me a second." He steps into the aisle to call somebody important.

I'm wearing control-top tights over control-top underwear. With Tim occupied, I breathe a little deeper, take a break from sucking in.

An old woman enters the theater, staggers up the steps. She's a bright spot in a lank dress, one arm bandaged at the bend. Loud blood beats in my ears. She's every frail grandma, every elderly aunt I never visit, every maternal figure who has loved me in spite of my selfishness. I use my mind to help her safely up the steps, all the way to Tim, who has finished his call. Authority teems from him, even without a stethoscope around his neck. The woman leans in close and asks him something, where is she, is this the right place? Tim gestures directions, waves her away. She starts down, afraid to push off from the handrail. She shimmers, the type of woman who makes you heart food from scratch, recites the recipe while you eat.

Tim comes back to his seat and sighs hard. "That lady's dumb nose touched my glasses," he says. He holds them out, shows me a smudge on the lens.

He's tired, a little cranky, maybe. I get back to the heads. "Is it like being a hairdresser?" I say. "Like you have to separate yourself or you'd be tortured by people's bad choices? Awful perms?"

"Maybe," Tim says. He uses his device to search for reviews of the film we are about to see. He reads them aloud. Tim has a voice that sounds like everything will be okay. It's a tone they must teach in med school.

"Rip-roaring," he says. "Hysterical but with heart."

Tim starts breathing slow during the previews. He's

snoring a little by the opening credits. I lean into him, pose his hot arm around my shoulder. I put my hand into our bucket of slippery popcorn. I don't tell Tim that I find movies in the theater confusing. The giant stars and their giant mouths are unsettling—the background actors unconvincing, living life with too much zeal. But I like *going* to the movies. I like plush seats and frigid air, all the dark snacking.

When I lose track of the plot, I lean away from sleeping Tim and reach into my huge, floppy purse. I feel around for contraband, one of the secret tallboys I picked up at the gas station. Onscreen, a bank teller insults the leading man while the dog pisses on a potted plant. I look at the descending theater heads and some of them start to flicker. I see a tiny black tunnel spiraling through one guy, his brain tissue eaten away and peppery in places. I guzzle the tallboy through a car chase and a madcap karate fight. I watch the sick, sparkly heads and hope these people can make peace with what's happening to them. I know there's nothing to be afraid of—death is just a countdown to the calm—but I'm doing that thing where I can't pull the oxygen from the air, where everything I look at gets smeary at the edges.

I drink and drink and focus on the threads coming together onscreen. The leading man is vindicated. The pug wears sunglasses and drives a car, its little paws on the steering wheel. I pop tallboy two. Tim's mouth falls open.

———

TIM MOVES THROUGH HIS rotations and I move along behind him, picking up shards of knowledge, trying to make sense of them. When he isn't exhausted, he entertains my questions.

"Pretend I'm a first-year," I say. "Leave nothing out."

I want to know about lumbar punctures, so Tim touches my spine while I brush my teeth. He uses his finger to dig into my lower back.

"This is the spot," he says. "Between L4 and L5. You draw a line from the iliac crest."

I've seen the crest he's talking about, that scooped bowl of bone on the hips of supermodels and centerfolds, but I've never seen mine. Tim is already dressed, a silver pen clipped to the pocket of his lab coat. He talks to my lumpy, naked reflection, raps his hard knuckle between my vertebrae.

"I'm amazed you can find a bone anywhere on me," I say.

I spit white foam into the sink. Tim says spinal taps are easier to perform on infants because their bones are still soft.

"Like a needle into butter," he says.

I shudder and ask if he's afraid of paralyzing a baby.

"Those itty-bitty bones!" I say. "Their wittle tiny backs! What if you mess it up?"

Tim tells me again he's the best in his class—there were no white blood cells in his last spinal.

"They call it a champagne tap," he says. "The chief resident buys you a bottle to celebrate."

He looks at his hand on my back and frowns.

"May I?" he says.

He pushes until his knuckles find the buried grooves in my spine. He works his fist up the column of bone, straightening me out as he goes. He rests his palm on the back of my neck, then braces his other forearm across my chest.

"What's this, the Heimlich?" I say. It's a rough kindness, this unexpected attention, and it flusters me.

Tim concentrates on shifting everything about me inward and upward. Once he's satisfied, he holds me in place, backs slowly away. My reflection looms in the foreground. He has made the difference in our heights obvious. I'm so much wider than Tim and now I'm taller, too. He assesses his work, finishes with an upward tilt of his head, which I mimic.

"Better," he says. "So much."

"I know, I know," I say, holding the pose.

"Don't shrink yourself," he says, serious. "Take up your space."

"Oh, that's no problem," I say. "That, I'm great at."

"Stop it," he scolds. "Don't put yourself down."

He steps in front of me and turns off the water, uses one of his monogrammed hand towels to dry the basin.

"Look at you!" he says. "I like it." Then, quietly, he says, "I like your size." And suddenly it's there, my size, this third person in the room with us.

Tim looks at himself in the mirror and shows his teeth. The steam from the running shower fogs up his glasses. He takes them off and uses his lab coat to rub the lenses. I start to slouch.

"Quit holding your breath," he says. "Don't lock your knees."

"There's no way this is how real people stand," I tell him. "It's exhausting."

"Good posture takes muscle memory and mental effort, both," Tim says. "Use your brain until your body gets it." Tim moves through the world like a human clipboard.

He goes to make the coffee, and I rush to take a shower. He says it's better if we leave at the same time. "That way we can enjoy each other's company in the car," he says. I don't have a key to his place.

In the car Tim plays the classic rock station. He slurps coffee from his thermos and steers with his knees. He floats through traffic, catching every green light. It's still dark when he drops me at my office. He parks head out in a handicap space and leans over me to open my door.

"Have a productive day, babe," he says, and taps my nose.

"You, too," I say. "Good luck with all the guts."

The car rises when I get out. Tim turns up the radio and powers down the windows. I use my big purse to hide my ass as I walk away.

I don't have a key to the office, either, so I go across the street to sit on the benches in the park. I eat a few bites of the toast Tim packed for me. He uses a plant sterol called Take Control! instead of butter. He says it's scientifically proven to lower cholesterol in rats. It tastes like ChapStick melted down. Eventually, I give up and throw hunks of bread at some birds. I peg one square in the chest, and it stands there, stunned.

Your size.

Tim is on a program of radical truth telling, and he says it's setting him free.

Nobody else is around—no moms with babies, no joggers jogging—so I tie my hair back and take out my one-hitter. It's another secret from Tim.

"Drinking is one thing," he tells me. "But pot keeps people from reaching their potential."

I get a little bit high, watch the world wake up.

There's a lit window at the Arby's where a cute cashier once mocked me for my big lunch order, ruining the place forever. I wonder if it's the same kid opening shop, if he's the one up early, cleaning grease traps, pushing a mop around. So many places have been wrecked for me. One mortifying moment triggers all the rest. It starts with fast food and radiates outward, a map of shame. Usually these thoughts make me feel like I'm being pushed to the ground, somebody's knee on my chest, but now I'm detached, each embarrassment an object resting in front of me, something to be picked up and weighed in my hand. That's the weed working.

There's the skating rink where a boy with fluorescent braces broke my teenage heart. There's the jagged sidewalk where I rolled my ankle and some asshole called out, "Timber!" as I fell. There's the public pool where I misinterpreted a friend's intense stare, his fingers grazing my bare shoulder.

"It was a mosquito!" he squawked, my hand already on his underwater dick.

I keep reloading the one-hitter. It's still so early. The weed I have is threaded through with little hairs. Colors start, everything gets pretty and crisp, exaggerated. There's something about how pot releases pressure in your eyeballs. Tim would know. Warm light slides around for a while. I blow smoke, and pink clouds stream across the sky.

After a while the birds get beady-eyed and silent, suddenly judgmental, cocking their heads to see me from different angles. The sunlit trees are too leafy, overwhelming. Crickets get rowdy in the bushes, and for a second I think the hood of my jacket is a person looming behind me.

"People respect the truth," Tim always says. I contemplate taping a note to the office door that says: *Got high. Got too high. Had to go home.* The birds finish my toast and then fly up and swarm with their friends, all of them swirling and looping into one big-ass bird.

When the coffee shop opens, I take a table by the window, lick lavender glaze off a doughnut. It's sublime. I flip through free circulars and wait for nine o'clock.

IRENE DRAGS ONE OF the lobby chairs up to my desk. I keep an eye out for Mr. Beezer, who doesn't like chitchat.

"Are vitamins a waste of money?" Irene asks. She uses one of her business cards to pick her teeth. "Because I heard you just pee them out."

She pulls a glob of plaque off the card, rolls it between her fingers.

"What about homeopathy?" she asks. "What does that even mean?"

I shouldn't have bragged to Irene about Tim, how he's a white-hot star being singled out for greatness in life.

"I don't know," I say. "I'll ask him."

Irene puts her business card back in the acrylic holder on my desk. Irene's cards are displayed behind Mr. Beezer's. Irene is Mr. Beezer's assistant. When I'm not answering phones or greeting visitors or making coffee, I am Irene's assistant.

The lobby is empty. A man's overcoat is draped across one of the couches.

Mr. Beezer's office door is closed and he's turned his line to "unavailable." Irene's door is open. A steady stream of AM talk drifts from the plastic radio on her desk. I trace the outline of my hand on company stationery.

"Ear candling's a joke, probably," Irene says, and scrapes at her fingernail polish with my letter opener. She makes a pile of red flakes by my stapler.

Irene's radio says, "Prices are slashed! Slashed! Slashed!"

She bites at a hangnail. "Ask him about gargling with salt water, too," she says. "I heard that's a scam. I heard the salt people made that up."

My pen is out of ink. I trace manic invisible circles on the message pad, the top of my desk, the back of my hand.

The phone rings, and I recite the greeting script. Mr. Beezer says the person on the other end can hear a smile, so I smile. Irene keeps looking at her nails, but she mouths along and smiles, too, toothy and deranged.

"It's for you," I say, and transfer the call to her office. She stands up and breaks into an awkward gallop. It's possible that Irene is slightly fatter than I am. She's shorter, and though my thighs are definitely smaller, my waist is maybe bigger. Tim says the eye prefers a 0.7 waist-to-hip ratio—there have been studies.

"I could care less," he'd said. "Or I couldn't care less, whichever. I mean ratios don't matter to me, obviously. It's just a fun fact."

Obviously.

It's possible the eye prefers Irene, even if she's bigger overall.

When Irene's door closes I use one of Mr. Beezer's cards to rake the red slivers of nail polish into the wastebasket. I move the chair back into place and make my pass through the lobby, situating a disrupted nesting table and hanging the overcoat on a brass hook. I pluck fuzz off an ottoman.

Mr. Beezer wants the lobby to feel like a living room, a place indicative of the homes he sells. Every morning, I float fresh rose petals in cut crystal bowls. I fluff throw pillows and spritz the room with cookie-scented air freshener. Unfortunately for Mr. Beezer, an office is still an office. The fluorescent light is harsh on the paisley wingbacks and brocade window treatments. The ceiling tiles are institutional. A copy machine dominates the north wall, its yellow extension cord trailing under the Oriental rug. My desk is the biggest giveaway, though I keep my wastebasket out of sight and hide my Kleenex box under a floral printed cover. It's too bad the clients don't see the room from behind my desk, where the perspective is slightly more convincing.

In the break room I rinse out coffee mugs in the sink. Irene comes in with one of Mr. Beezer's files.

"This wasn't in the right place," she says. "Not even close."

"Oh, no," I say. I turn off the water and dry my hands on my skirt. "I'm so sorry."

Tim keeps telling me to stop being so sorry for everything all the time.

"I don't apologize for anything, ever," he says. And it's true, he doesn't.

Irene moves in so close the space between us is now charged, tight enough to be slapping space or hugging space. I can't think of any recourse, so I brace myself for something unwelcome, whatever it is. All Irene does is cup her mouth and stage-whisper, "This caused us a lot of embarrassment. We looked extremely unprofessional."

"Okay," I say. "I didn't realize."

Irene shifts her weight and stares at me. Bright peach gloss congeals in the corners of her mouth.

"Look," she says. "Your job isn't only phones. Reception is more than that."

I know what my job is. Irene knows I know what my job is.

"I see what you mean," I say. There are only so many things you can say when you should be saying you're sorry.

Irene puts the file on the countertop.

"Beezer is so far up my ass," she says. She closes her eyes and squeezes the bridge of her nose. She sidesteps me and pours herself a cup of coffee, dumps in an avalanche of powdered cream.

"Just use your brain, please?" she says. She's Irene again, aggressively friendly, helping me to be better.

"The first rule of filing," she says, "is nothing comes before something. You should know that."

"You're right," I say. "I should."

TIM CALLS AT LUNCH. I'm eating at my desk, a cheeseburger and fries in the open top drawer, stacks of Mr. Beezer's files all around. I shoulder the phone, correct mistakes as I go along. "Meyer Realty Group" before "Myerson, Elliott" and "Park Vista Condominiums" before "Parker Estates." Tim tells me the first-year anatomy students couldn't find a cadaver with a uterus. He says four out of five women who donate their bodies to science have had hysterectomies.

"They have what's called a blind-ending pouch," Tim says. "It's exactly what it sounds like."

He tells me the first-years will have to complete their studies on female pigs. I lose my place in the alphabet.

"You're kidding," I say.

A stray piece of paper floats out of the file cabinet and onto the floor.

"No, it's true," Tim says.

The paper slips all the way under my desk, where I will have to crawl and smoosh myself around to get to it. *Fuck filing*. Just like that I'm done with administrative duties for the day. I merge the contents of two unrelated accounts and cram them into the cabinet. I drop the empty folder into the trash. I'll shred everything later, leave no evidence.

"I mean, I could understand a monkey, maybe," I say. "But this is ridiculous."

Tim is quiet, and I can hear the hospital loudspeaker fizzing on his end.

"I'm just saying there are, like, implications."

"Pig anatomy is really very close to ours," Tim says. He sounds tired. "Nearly all major structures are the same."

"But not exactly," I say. "They aren't exactly the same." I shove thick stacks of files into the space at the back of the alphabet.

"Of course not," he says. "But they have to take what they can get. Everyone is disappointed."

We hang up, and I finish my food. I fish out every last fry from the warm, greasy bag.

Irene stands at the copy machine, backlit by a periodic flash. I've got a food buzz—my vision is gauzy.

I stare into the fluorescence of the lobby and imagine Tim among the first-year students. I picture him lifting sheet after sheet with growing disappointment. He catalogs the women by sight, moving between their open bodies.

———

MR. BEEZER LEAVES EARLY. I leave when Irene leaves. She takes the fat ring of keys from her purse and locks up while I wait behind her.

"Give me some room," she says, elbows jutting.

"Have a great night," I say when she heads to her car. She puts both thumbs up and keeps walking.

I smoke on my way to the bus stop, past the spoiled Arby's and Mr. Beezer's dry cleaner, past Pegasus Plaza and a gross motel Tim calls the Sexual Asphyxiation Inn, where people are always throwing bottles of piss out the windows and setting each other on fire.

There's a crust punk by the entrance, leaning against bulletproof glass. I pass him all the time, but now I notice he has a cast on one leg. His toes poke out, wrinkled and covered in some kind of dark gunk. His eyes are milky. He shakes an amber bottle of pills at me, hisses a price. I fight the urge to give him everything in my wallet, to drop to my knees and sign my name on the plaster, dot my "i" with a little heart. He's dazzling under the streetlights—so pitiful and pretty he may as well be wrapped in tinsel.

MY BUS RUNS IN a loop—the population swells downtown. I'm killing time, waiting for Tim's shift to end.

The aisles are filled with commuters holding leather straps. The turns are wide and everyone sways together. No one tries to sit on the sliver of seat next to me. "Keep it moving," the driver says to the swarming rush-hour bodies.

A woman in a hairnet scratches her neck. A red patch slinks under her shirt collar, disappears at her ear, reappears on her cheek. Her skin is dry and coarse but not peeling. Eczema? Psoriasis? Tim would know. He would warn her against starch, against detergent and perfume. He would snap on a pair of latex gloves, spread her thick with antibiotic cream.

At Greenville Avenue, a delivery boy replaces the itchy woman. He looks through his orders and chooses a Styrofoam container, throws strands of some poor customer's lo mein into his mouth. There is a faint mark, a white star, in the hollow at the boy's throat. It's a trach scar. If Tim had to, if things got desperate, he would use my Beezer Homes pen to reopen the star, save the boy from choking to death. All the bus people would applaud, insist on celebration. The driver would detour and double-park, hazards flashing. The crowd would carry their hero to the nearest bar.

The bus stops again, empties out. The delivery boy and I watch Tim's parade from the window. With everyone gone, there is only the sound of new air, wet and frantic, rushing through the boy's throat.

I'VE MISSED HAPPY HOUR by a long shot—everyone is drunk and in various states of collapse. It's a dive, a last resort. The ceiling is tiled with license plates, and the bar taps are gearshifts. A bald woman licks salt out of her palm and takes a shot of tequila, smiles at me through a wedge of lime.

I sit next to her and watch the reflection of her curved skull behind rows of liquor. She's painted golden eyebrows onto her forehead. I wonder if there's a wig in her purse.

The jukebox starts playing a song everybody knows, one that has its own dance.

"Come on," the bald woman says, and pokes me in the arm. "Shake your shit." She dances in place on the barstool, her little hands up in the air.

"Give me cheap," I tell the bartender.

I shoot quick doubles, gin poured from the plastic bottle. I think of icebreakers, pleasantries, but the words fall away. The bald woman and I don't talk, but we are sharing space now, getting to where we're going. She lights little books of bar matches, burns them down, and shakes them out. My ass is aching—there is no barstool suitable for it—but the drinks are helping, like when your eyes adjust to a dim room.

"What kind of cancer do you have?" I ask.

"Excuse me?" she says, and looks behind her, like I'm talking to somebody else.

"I mean, obviously, right?" I say to her.

"What a fucking question," she says. She talks around the matchbook in her teeth.

"It's not lung, is it?" I ask. "Can I see your fingernails? Have they overrun your cuticles?" I glance at the woman's hands on the bar top. She draws them into little fists. "Are they spreading around the edges and meeting on the other side? Is your urine gray?"

"Ha," the woman says. "No."

She shakes her head and fumbles with the matches. She strikes one and lets the whole book go up. Her face is terrible in the flash.

"I'm interested because I'm a doctor," I tell her. "I'm a medical doctor, so these things interest me."

"Well, shit," the bald woman says. "A doctor."

"I'm a heart doctor," I explain. "But I treat cancer patients, too. There's a lot of overlap."

"Cardiologist," the bald woman says. "You're a cardiologist." She laughs.

"Yeah," I say. "Yep. What about you?"

"I'm on disability," she says. "I do what I want."

"Amazing," I say. "Enjoy it."

Down the bar a man is slumped over, sleeping.

"Surgery, surgical procedures," I tell the woman. "I'm a doctor."

"Right," she says.

"It's really rewarding," I say. "It's a rewarding career."

"I don't think I'd have the stomach for it, personally," she says. "For cutting people open."

"Part of the job," I say. "Gets to be routine. Like a doorman opening a door."

"Sounds like you've got every little thing figured out," she says.

She flashes fingers at the bartender. Her wrists are delicate things. A neon sign casts her fine collarbones in blue light. If it weren't for the woman's head, she could be a model. I asked Tim once if there were any hot cadavers, any beautiful bodies who donated themselves to science.

"That's sick," he'd said. "You're sick." But he had laughed a little. "Don't tell me you're jealous of dead people now, too."

The bartender pours our round slow and loose—runoff pools on the bar. Carpal tunnel, maybe.

"Bone cancer," the woman says when the bartender is out of earshot. "But it started in my pussy."

"Oh, bone?" I say. "That's no problem."

The woman slaps both her palms on the bar top, shaking caddies and highballs, scattering salt into her lap.

"Is that so?" she says, and hoots. The sound comes from behind her head, from somewhere else. She brings up her drink in a toast. "In your opinion, bone cancer's no big deal?"

"That's right," I say, and clink the lip of the woman's glass. "In my professional opinion, you're going to be just fine."

TIM TELLS ME DOCTORS make the best lovers. "It's anatomy," he says. "It's just knowing where things are."

He tells me this during my breast exam. He wears his little white lab coat. I'm high and naked, and Tim is thorough, slow, his glasses off.

"Let's see what else we have," he says, and gets down on his knees. His face is so small next to my body.

He inspects me an inch at a time with his hands, his mouth. He moves up my thighs.

"You've got a lot of ground to cover," I say.

"Don't start," he says.

He spreads me apart and points out markers. He says, "This is the labium majus . . . and the minus."

He describes me in words I've never heard before—some that sound good and some that sound horrible, like poetry or caught phlegm, depending. It's the hairy weed that's freaking me out, making everything sinister.

Tim touches my cervix with his finger. I know it's my cervix he touches because he gets excited and tells me, "This is your cervix, Sheila."

"Okay," I say. "Enough."

But he doesn't stop. He continues to chart me, pushes upward until I feel something in a strange place, a place that hasn't been or shouldn't be touched. It's impossible, what he does with his hand. He says the word "vault" and then, softer, the word "vestibule." I think of the space between two closed doors.

When he's finished with me, Tim goes to the sink. There are twenty-eight planes of the hand, and Tim washes all of them. He's told me over and again what the parts are, but I can never remember—the four sides of each finger, the tops of them. The palm is divided into three sections, maybe. There are dorsals, flexors; the words tumble out too quickly.

"It's rote at this point," Tim says. "I don't even think about it."

I stand at the sink behind him, as straight as I can manage. "I like watching you do it."

"It's just how we scrub in," he explains.

When I wash my hands, I count, too. I get to twenty-four, maybe twenty-six planes. I'll never figure it out. This is how you make someone love you—you teach them something memorable about something boring, something they must do every day for the rest of their life.

"When you leave me," I tell Tim, "I'll be stuck with wet hands, counting forever, getting it all wrong."

A MAN PUKES BLOOD in the lobby. It doesn't look like blood, but blood doesn't look like blood when it's in puke. Blood looks gritty, like coffee grounds. I don't tell the man this when I bring the box of tissues over from my desk. This is my chance to be a calming presence.

The man's wife holds my wastebasket under his dripping chin. They are newly married and building their first home. The wife says it's possible nerves are to blame.

When black liquid begins to come out fast, the man stands up and spins around, trying to outrun the problem. He covers his mouth with his hands, but instead of stopping the flow, he pressurizes it. Irene, who is sweetly correcting herself for something in Mr. Beezer's office, steps out in time to see the pukey projection, the distance. She stops in the doorway, her hands in her hair.

"Oh my God," she says.

I should love my body more. It carries my soul around, lets me taste food and get high and come, and it never pulls shit like this.

The man and his wife will have to reschedule. The wife apologizes before pushing her husband through the double doors. His crumpled black tissues trail through the lobby.

"Sheila," Irene says from the doorway, "something has to be done about this."

"I know," I say, and watch the black circles seeping into the throw pillows, ruining the rehearsal home.

The lobby is an extension of me, and I am an extension of Mr. Beezer. There isn't really a way to prepare for something like this, to clean up something that belongs inside someone else. I am composed, collected, handling the situation.

TIM TELLS ME HE wants to spend the night alone.

"Can I put my panties on before you kick me out?" I say.

"Funny," he says. He kisses me, but it's perfunctory. He yawns. "It's been such a long day."

"It's so early," I say.

He tells me a patient his group has been following was lost forever under deep anesthesia.

"Jesus, that's awful," I say. "Do you want to talk about it?" I touch his hand, turn toward him in bed.

"It was a fluke," Tim says. "Nobody's fault." He says he learned a lot: how to pronounce time of death, how to fill out morgue forms.

"The paperwork is insane," he says. He fluffs his pillow, flips the blankets down on my side to let me out.

A sad sigh comes out of me before I can stop it.

"Babe," he says. "Everything's fine. But I need to recharge."

"Can't I help you relax?" I say. I hate the desperate catch in my voice, the frantic feeling I get when he needs space. "No talking, I swear. I'll read over here."

I pick up one of his textbooks, flip to a full-color spread of warts on a foot. I sit at his desk, switch on the reading lamp.

"You don't want to read my derm book, babe," he says. "Trust me."

"You really want me to go?" I say. I stand up and put my dress on slowly, dramatically buttoning each button to give him a chance to reconsider. He doesn't. I wad my tights into a ball and shove them into my purse.

"I guess I'll go out drinking," I say. I'm picking a fight.

"Drink if you want, read if you want," Tim says flatly. "Just not here, okay?"

I ask again why he's even with me.

"Because you're so independent," he deadpans. I feel my face fall. He gets out of bed, wraps his arms around the biggest part of me. He's sorry, in his way.

"You're funny, for one thing," he says. "Funny equals smart."

"I'm no M.D.," I say. I let myself sink into him, try to store this feeling for later. "I'm no R.N. or EMT. I've got none of the letters."

"There are lots of different types of intelligence, babe," he murmurs into my hair.

"That's something smart people say to dumb people," I say.

THE WORLD TILTS, AND all is gray and churning, silvery bile. The bartender is stern, mad at me for something. I move through the bar like a sow on roller skates, people part the way. A pretty girl with a lazy eye holds open the bathroom door for me, and I duck under her arm, grateful.

I shutter myself in a stall and slam down on the toilet. Something cracks in the tank behind me, and there is a sound like water spraying somewhere inside the wall. *Oh, well.* Even when I'm sober, I don't have the quads for hovering.

The spins don't feel circular to me—there's a kind of visual stutter, a section of the bathroom stall that keeps rewinding. It's more interesting than nauseating, but I have to grab on to the sanitary receptacle box to steady myself. The box is cold metal, jutting out into the stall. Some wrongheaded curiosity compels me to lift the lid and look inside. It's soaked tampons and pads, exactly what I expected, all the way down to the smell.

The door swings open and music rushes in. Clicking heels and water running in the sink, women talking about a man. Then one of them is pushing on my stall, the door creaking open. Even shit-faced, I raise my leg automatically, foot out quick to snap the stall door closed.

"I'm in here!" I say.

The woman says, "Sorry, honey!" and backs away.

My bar reflexes are supreme, something to behold. *Atta girl,* I think.

I'M NOT SURE IF it's the crack of my beer tab or the scattered laughter that stirs Tim awake. This is a makeup date, Tim's treat. It's a gross-out comedy, guys who slap each other's dicks and lose a suitcase full of money. There's a subplot where a teenager tries to get laid, has diarrhea. I'm good and drunk in the dark theater.

It's crowded, a sold-out show. There are tumors growing in almost everyone, too many to count. If it isn't cancer, it's some cardiovascular mishap in the works: there's yellowy gunk building up in one guy, a cholesterol boat ready to sail into his bloodstream. But I'm looking past the glow, letting giant idiots entertain me. I know that for each head that twinkles there is one waiting to light up. Months or years from now some spark will catch and flare. It's too much to keep track of.

Tim's eyes fly open. He takes one look at an overflowing toilet onscreen and titters along with the rest of the audience. There's a jump cut to an angry woman in lingerie, trapped in the trunk of a car. People crack up, slap their thighs. Tim has zero context but busts out laughing anyway. He leans over, elbows me a little, makes sure I've caught the joke. And I want to believe him, I do. That he knows exactly what's happening, that he's been right here with me the entire time.

I TAKE THE BUS in circles, pass Tim's stop over and over. Each time the bus driver could break the pattern, leave the loop and go somewhere else, but he never does.

"We're not on a track," I shout. "We're free to move about the city."

A lady across the aisle from me takes her baby and moves to a seat in the back. I close my eyes and let the side of my face smash against the window. Elm Street, Malcolm X, Fair Park. The bus stops and stops.

I see the hospital. "My friend has bone cancer," I yell to the driver. "Let me out."

The bus door opens and sidewalk rushes up. I sit on concrete for a while, wait for my second wind.

The revolving door is a bitch. The elevator buttons make no sense.

"This is a pressing matter," I tell the skinny nurse behind the counter. I put my palm on the open book in front of her. "Pressing."

The nurse says Tim's name over the loudspeaker. When he comes to the front, she shrugs. He walks toward me, sees what the fear is doing to my face.

"She can't be here," the nurse says.

"I've got it," Tim says to her.

The nurse says, "She gotta go. You want me to get the doctor? She gotta leave."

"Donna," Tim snaps, "relax." The nurse puts her hands on her hips, walks back behind the counter.

Tim steers me down the hall. He takes me to the call room and closes the door behind us.

He says, "What are you doing here?"

In a panic, I ask him to find my liver.

"It may be enlarged," I say.

"Did you take something?" Tim says. "What did you take?"

"Crust punk pill," I say.

"What?" Tim says. "What did you say?"

"This is your bed?" I collapse on the bottom bunk. "It's like camp," I say. "Camp Cut-You-Up."

"You're drunk," Tim says.

"I'm lots of things," I say.

"You can't be here," Tim says.

"Do other people sleep here with you?" I ask. "Female people?"

"What are you talking about?" Tim says.

I say, "There's something wrong with me, you know. *Internally.*"

Tim sighs and lifts my blouse. He pushes on my gut.

"You're fine. No abnormalities."

He looks straight ahead and palpates, does that thumping thing doctors do. He tells me he can't feel anything.

"You're sure," I say. "You don't feel anything . . . off?" I'm getting belligerent. My voice is so loud.

"Sheila, stop," Tim says. "Here."

He puts his hand over mine and moves it along my body.

He pushes me into myself. "Your bladder," he says, "no lumps, no masses." He moves my hands around behind. "These are your kidneys," he says. He presses my fingers in, makes sure I can feel the edges of what he describes. "Okay?" he says. "Okay?"

"Please," I say. "Only you can help me feel better."

Tim stands up and looks at me. He locks the door. He takes off his glasses, rests them on a little table. He pushes me back on the bed, pulls my blouse open. I let myself be posed, positioned. He tugs my skirt off, my tights, frees me from my enormous bra. He crouches with a knee on either side of me.

"Here," he says. He puts his face deep into my cleavage, pushes my tits up and around his ears.

"Yes," I say, "yes."

At the same time, his fingers are moving inside me, his hand.

"Your ovaries," he says. He presses his little ear flat against my chest. He listens.

"Your heart," he says.

"Find more," I say.

IN OUR CIRCLE

IF SHE WAS AFRAID OF us, she never let on. She'd pull her chair right into our bloody-minded circle, get dirty up to her wrists. It didn't matter if we pinched pots or rolled out dicks and balls, at the end of each class the art shrink would take whatever we'd made and mash it back in on itself. We'd watch her small hands choke through the mess and try not to levitate the craft table with our peckers.

"It's a process," she told us.

Of course there would be threats and thrown elbows, sometimes somebody getting grabbed by the throat. When this happened the art shrink would sigh and push the call button. The doctors would rush in, their little clipboards up like shields. The rest of us sat still, hands soft where everyone could see.

"Allow these distractions to deepen your concentration," the art shrink said.

When they let me out, I was just as mad as when I went in, only fatter and too lazy to exercise my wrath. Plus, I'd shaved my eyebrows off for no real reason, and what grew back was fine and blond and seemed to endear the world to me. I'd done the work and passed their tests, but my mind was still snarled.

They set me up in a halfway house in Abilene, right near the air force base. Guys in camo trawled around, looking strict. On weekends the jets pulled endless hot laps, rattling the light bulbs and shaking the windowpanes.

To keep the red thoughts away, I bought myself a card table, a couple tubs of modeling clay. Now I make little ball-people and smoosh them down. A thousand snakes, warped pancakes. I think about the art shrink, how she told a roomful of monsters to leave space for luminous moments. I squish that thick stuff around, contemplate my talents, wonder if this is what she meant.

GLOW HUNTER

BO'S MORE BRIGHTLY LIT THAN the rest of us. "Charisma" is the word. It's the reason her sneezes are so compelling, why she's able to walk barefoot everywhere and it doesn't seem disgusting. Or it's chemicals, maybe, sneaky little messages her body puts out. The world seems to spread open for her. As a child, she clambered onto the small stages of her hometown—she was an Annie and a Scarecrow, an understudy to a Tinker Bell. She's really not much of an actress, but she enchants people just the same. I've seen strangers stop what they're doing to watch her shake sugar into her tea.

_____

BO SAYS SHE CAN guarantee my first psychedelic experience will be exquisite. "Set" is short for "mind-set," and Bo says ours needs to be curious and playful, open to what will come. For the setting, she says we'll need to be somewhere soft, preferably with access to nature. "The ideal is, like, inside a tent full of stuffed animals, on a raft at sea," she says. "But a car works, too."

"YOU THINK MAMA MIGHT like this?" Bo drawls. She holds up a truck stop trinket, something lead painted and Texas themed, assembled by tiny, faraway hands. She wants people to think we're sisters—the guy pumping our gas, the server at a doughnut place. I'm not crazy about this, but it's fun for her, something to break up the dull, gaping highway. We've been killing the last days of summer with drives through the worst parts of this state. Bo's mom is a free-range type, but my curfew keeps us tethered. We've seen everything worth seeing and plenty that isn't—the bat caverns and the toilet seat museum, that big-ass hole in the ground where a supercollider is supposed to go. She'd never admit it, but Bo cares a great deal what mamas of all kinds might think—we both do—even this fake one she has conjured in the moment.

BO PLAYS HER GAMES. "We grew up on an alpaca farm," she says, this time to a cashier, a kid with a rattail. "We come from a long line of wool people," she says. I tilt my head and squint at her. "Fur people?" she tries. I snort. She tells the guy we've got yarn in our blood, that we're on our way to see a man about a loom.

I'M SISTER TO TOO many already—descending boy versions of me with buzzed hair and Adam's apples, sharp little jaw-lines. My house smells like feet and ballsack, and I can't sleep in a room that's quiet. Every morning when I leave, my mom says, "Have fun!"—the implication being that she can't, so I might as well.

I CAN TELL THE cashier is already deep in Bo's thrall, watching her lips for shapes, not words. "Actually," I say, "she's an only child. And we don't know dick about alpacas." I'm harsh in my head, though I'm usually shy with strangers—I "sir" and "ma'am" them—but Bo makes me brave.

JEFF TOLD ME, "NO matter how hot she is, someone, some-where, is sick of her shit."

I was calm when he said it, or I'd tried to be. It was the first time I'd been inside his house in so long. His particular circumstance seemed to warrant a visit, but I'd mostly come to check on Linda, his mom, to see how his fuckup was affecting her. I was disappointed that she was at work, jealous of the customers who got to see her kind face, bask in her warmth. Jeff and I sat on opposite ends of his couch but were in the same helicopter onscreen, blowing stuff up with our swivel M60s. His phone kept buzzing in his pocket and we both knew it was Bo, frantic, on the other end.

"That sounds like men's rights garbage," I said. I could feel him staring, but I focused on our strategy, destroying enemy health packets we'd found hidden in a culvert.

"Men, women, whatever," Jeff said, so smug.

"Because you know so much about relationships," I said. I shot up a bunch of civilian huts just because. People ran out in bloody pairs with their hands up, and I shot them some more. "You're so wise, in general," I said. "You've made some really great decisions." People fell to the ground and flickered, then they disappeared.

MY MOM HAS BEEN wiping asses for a decade. Her life is laundry and boxes of macaroni, lice combs and digging raisins out of the couch. She'll come into my room and sit on my bed. She'll touch my hand, ask how my day was, then nod off as I answer. I can't even blame her for it.

"WE'RE TWINS," BO SAYS. "If you can't tell."

I say, "We're not." It's just mean to invite the comparison—who can beat that bone structure?

"Imagine me blond," she says to the rattail kid. She puts

her head against my head, pulls the veil of my lank hair across her face. Blond sounds better than what I've got—khaki is more apt. "Wait," she says, covers her dark eyebrows with her fingers.

"Stupid," I say, laughing, batting her hand away. "Stop it." The last thing I want is to be related to Bo. I want her to tell the truth to this cashier, make him fuck off forever, but what Bo and I have going on—this electric *something*—I'm not sure either of us knows exactly what to call it.

BO SAYS THESE FARM routes hypnotize her, that if she stops talking she'll fall into a road coma and kill us both. "Jeff used to sit where you are, snoring. I'd get bored. Every song on the radio was like a lullaby, and I started to believe those rumble strips on the shoulders of the road were some kind of braille, a message from the great beyond I could read by driving on it. You know what the beyond said to me? It just said, 'Go to sleep. Go to sleep. Go to sleep.' "

THREE NIGHTS AGO, BO and I were sleeping on my living room floor when she swiped at me with her cold foot. My name was in her mouth, different from how I'd ever heard it. I'd been dreaming about her right then, and the sound of her real-life voice made me feel crazy, like my skull was porous, the fantasy oozing out. "Is there somewhere we can go?" she whispered.

"You mean *elsewhere*?" I said, and the word was loaded, code for whatever was about to happen between us. You can't just wish for something and really get it, can you? But a list of things I'd been noticing rolled through me: Bo sitting so close to me all the time, sometimes needing my help to put sunscreen on her back, asking me to smell her perfumed wrist and say what I thought.

I was up fast, tugging her hand, afraid she'd evaporate. There was the sound of brothers breathing, stirring, as we ran through the slotted dark. Out of the living room and down the hall. Into the bathroom, the only room in my house with a lock. The toilet was running for no reason, some problem with the tank. The shadows of familiar things: little toothbrushes all in a row by the sink, brown plunger on a square of newsprint in a corner. Elsewhere. We stripped our T-shirts off like we were about to jump into a pool, dropped them in a pile on the fuzzy sea-foam bath mat. Me, trying to speed things up and slow them down all at once. Bo, on her knees in front of me. "You'll like it," she said, a fact. She hugged me around my waist, kissed a mosquito bite on my hip. Me asking, "Is this for real?" and Bo smiling, saying, "Didn't you know this was coming?" *No fucking way. Never in a million years.* We had the window open, sticky air sailing through. I sat on the lip of the grimy tub with my hands in her hair, bath toys everywhere, towels drip-dripping on the rod. Her ribs were gold in the streetlight. All of that happened to me, which means it could happen again.

———

ASK BO WHY SHE didn't make it to Hollywood and she'll blame her mom for not hauling her to auditions and shoving her in front of more cameras when she was little. We circle back to mothers a lot, because Bo hates hers and because I love mine, maybe a little too much. "Also, I never got famous because of these," she says, and clicks her teeth together. She points out that they could have been fixed had her mom been better with money after her dad left. Also, her mom has bad teeth, which Bo had inherited.

"So, you're saying you never made it as an actress because of your mother and your mother and your mother?" I'm teasing, but I worry sometimes that Bo is one of those women who hates women.

Bo says, "She *named* me after her, if that tells you anything about how bonkers she is."

"Men do that all the time," I say. "They call it tradition."

IF OUR DAILY GOAL is driving to underwhelming tourism, cow shit is our summerlong pursuit, or rather finding the mushrooms that grow in it. It hasn't rained in weeks—it's not going to—but there's the threat, damp and close as a hug, and we've heard humidity alone is enough to coax the little guys out. Every time Bo gets a feeling about a particular pasture, she pulls over, encourages me to duck under barbed wire and snoop around. She's deemed me the designated gatherer, says I'm the clear choice. She mentions my Honors Chem class, the fact that I'll be premed in the fall. She stays behind, lazy and gorgeous, smoking on the hood of her car while I go hunt in shit.

BO IS ALWAYS DANGLING new universes, places she says are hidden in plain sight. I already feel high when she's around—giddy, tingles on my scalp. Once, I let her drag me to a trailer park psychic. A woman in a leotard told me my aura was dingy, that I could pay her extra to hose it off with her mind. I've told Bo I don't want to turn into a fractal elf or watch my hands pool into liquid rainbows. She tells me not to worry, that with mushrooms we'll be us, only better. She calls this my Summer of Yes. "Imagine everything slightly dazzling," she says, "real life with a glow."

HOW DO I GET it to happen again?

BO'S CAR SMELLS LIKE weed and her body lotion, some heavy berry bullshit I'd normally hate. She drives like she talks—fast and distracted, veering off to weird places. She's got her hair cropped close, slicked back with the same shea butter that makes her collarbones gleam. Not long ago she chopped her long ponytail off with kitchen scissors. She claims she did it because she needed something soft yet shocking to throw in her mother's face during an argument. "It shut her right up," Bo said, but if my breakup math is right, Bo really cut her hair because of Jeff. She tells lies like this. She showed it to me, the jagged tail, black and lustrous in a Ziploc bag she keeps, for some reason, in the trunk of her car.

"Aren't you gonna donate it to the little bald kids?" I asked.

"Fuck no, that belongs to me," she said. "I'll use it in a curse or on a puppet or something." Bo's doing a gap year instead of college in the fall—she has a lot of projects going on, all at once.

"LET'S SEE," BO SAYS. "What don't you know already?" Her favorite flowers are birds-of-paradise. "Any plant with a beak gets my vote," she says. She thinks tomatoes are goopy, too wet to eat. If she decides to get a tattoo, it will be a full backpiece, an inky-black sky with constellations in the negative space, a shooting star, maybe a fluorescent UFO. "Stay blank or go big," she says.

BO SWEARS THAT SOFTY cigarettes are ever-so-slightly longer and that boxes are too pointy in the waistband of her shorts, poking her every time she bends or stretches or kicks or twirls. She says she's measured, in centimeters and in puffs both. Plus, she likes that you can gouge a hole in the top of the pack, tap your finger on the bottom, and up pops a single smoke—a little miracle. Bo really has only one wrong tooth, and it's cute. It's in the middle on the bottom, ruined from nicotine, twisted and a little taller than the others, death colored.

I'M USUALLY NERVOUS IN cars. Whether I'm driving or riding, I can't seem to forget that I'm in a little shell, hurtling along. I want a death that comes from the inside, something I won't have to watch as it's happening—a clot turned loose in my blood, a glossy organ seizing up and shuddering in secret. Car wrecks are splattered windshields and jutting bones, the listless highway patrol scooping bits of you and not-you off the asphalt, zipping the whole mess into a bag. But when Bo is driving—even though she's always looking at herself in the rearview or swerving around road trash in case it's a bag of kittens—my anxiety, usually a thrum as steady and constant as my heartbeat, is something I can smother, tamp down, forget about for a while.

BO'S DONE MUSHROOMS LOTS of times with Jeff, but my experience is limited to the little white buttons my mom chops up for spaghetti dinners. I'm not sure I could even identify a shiitake in a lineup.

WHENEVER THERE'S A LULL, we swing back to Jeff. It's an odd topic, but he's what we have most in common. "What made him pick 'Jeff,' do you think?" Bo asks. Outside her window, tan nothing rushes on forever. Jeff's family named themselves when they first came to the U.S.—just passed around a big book and decided. His father chose "David" and his mother chose "Linda." Jeff was Jeff, obviously, but his older sister, in a move Bo and I agree really showed some pizzazz, decided on "Candy."

"He thought he was picking "Jif," like the peanut butter," I say.

"That makes so much sense," she says.

I'm the authority on Early Jeff. I grew up seeing his kitchen window from mine, watching him do his homework at his dining room table every weeknight. His phone number is one of the few I know by heart. Jeff's parents were scientists in their country. They worked with robots and vaccines. Now they sell T-shirts and magic tricks and plastic bullshit from their kiosk at the mini-mall.

"They've been importing this spray called Liquid Ass," Bo tells me. She's the Current Jeff expert. "I'm serious!" she says. "The translation on the bottle says, 'And it will burst and stinky will full the air.' "

I'm dying. "It does not!" I say.

Bo says, "Stinky. Will. Full."

"Why would a thing like that exist?" I say, gasping. Bo's true laugh is almost nothing, just this sweet little clicking noise in her throat.

———

I KNEW JEFF SOLD pot, everybody did, though I never imagined he'd get into any trouble for it. Our town is plagued by more serious stuff—black tar heroin coming up from Mexico, Oxy coming in from everywhere. The police had dogs prowling the halls, sniffing at lockers. They found Jeff's weed inside a split-open tennis ball. To me, this seemed like bad luck, his hiding place as clever as any. "How can somebody so smart be so stupid?" Bo said later. "I mean, have either of you ever *met* a dog?" I took Jeff's spot as salutatorian and tried not to be too thrilled about that. I'd been having feelings I was ashamed of for a while. Besides being incredibly smart, Jeff was popular, something that baffled me. We still studied together, but not much more. He slid around in every social circle, welcomed by everyone. I was jealous—of the people who got to have Jeff, the people he got to have. Bo told me she and Jeff were already having problems before he got busted. "It was running its course," she said. This is Jeff's Summer of the Ankle Monitor, Bo's Summer of No Jeff.

BO DRIVES US THROUGH cut-up flatlands—cotton, cows, cotton, cows—waiting for her fungal intuition to light up. She refuses to take I-45 because of something Linda told her. "It's stupid," she says, "but it's habit." In Chinese, the number 4 is the same as the word for death. Over there your address could be death-oh-death Whatever Street or you work on the deathy-death floor of your building. But no, Bo says she heard that's not even the case anymore. Because it is such a bad omen, Linda's people, as a nation, have now done away with fours altogether.

"Wait, what?" I ask. Bo says it's no different from what we do here, with high-rises and the number 13—we skip that unlucky floor, or pretend to. I ask her: Wouldn't it be easier to just give death a different name? Bo's not sure.

"Cheeto," she says, and opens her mouth for me. I feed her a few, then hold a red straw to her lips.

WHAT'S WEIRDER, TALKING ABOUT Jeff or talking about Jeff's mom? We're both obsessed with Linda: how warm she is, how available. We love her tiny shoulders and her big, fluffy hair. How she holds your hands in her hands when you talk to her. "She's the best listener," I say. Then I add, "Probably." Linda's English isn't great, which makes things, somehow, less complicated.

Bo says, "I bought one of those language kits, to try to come at her from her side, but I'm so terrible. We do a lot of hand gestures." Bo tells me Linda has been wearing a little bandanna around her neck, and we squeal about how adorable. "Every time she sees me, she just lights up," Bo says. "Moms usually hate me."

Too quickly I say, "Mine doesn't." Bo smiles and raises her eyebrows at me.

BO IS BACKLIT BY the big opal sky, her good hand on the wheel. We hold eye contact for the first time in a long while. I see that she's checking on me, watching my face for a twitch of worry. It's nowhere. I mimic her bemused expression, her cool confidence.

BO AND I WEREN'T exactly friends in school—we were polite. It was Jeff who shoved us together. Bo, this strange girl who made abysmal grades and covered her arms in highlighter filigree. She'd wait in the library while Jeff and I did homework, cutting holes in her clothes or vandalizing desks with her bizarre poems. Sometimes the two of them would take a break and go out to her car to get high. I'd study spitefully, prepare to kick Jeff's ass on whatever test. They'd come back stoned and giddy, sticky heat radiating. I'd never smelled sex before. I could have stormed off, but I didn't—I'd sit there wallowing in the hot tang of them, not used to being in such proximity to what I wanted.

AS LITTLE KIDS, JEFF and I shared a dream journal, a sketchbook we filled with monsters and nonsense, the weird cathedrals we wandered through. We passed it back and forth between our houses, slept with it close to our heads.

HERE'S A DIFFERENT CASHIER, mouth gaping, equally enthralled. I ask him for a Band-Aid for Bo's bleeding palm. "Jesus," he says when she holds it up for him. "How'd you do that?"

"Mystery gash," she says, and shrugs, shoves her dripping red fist back into the pocket of her cutoffs.

She got sliced up doing parking lot cartwheels, but she wants to seem dangerous. This cashier isn't much older than us—still, he puts a kink in his brow. He's trying hard to project maturity and wisdom. Underneath, he's all creep. They don't sell bandages, so he rushes off to grab the first-aid kit. "And cigarettes," Bo reminds him. She smokes menthols even though she says they're full of fiberglass and grit, that they make her feel like she's got glitter in her lungs. It's the same reason she loves hot sauce and cinnamon gum, those breath mints with the supernova centers—she likes to feel a sting. Salem is her brand of choice, and she calls cigarettes her "little witches."

Bo spins a wire rack of postcards—cactuses, cowboys. She holds up one of a bikini lady with a python draped over her shoulders. "What do you think about this look, Sis? Could I pull this off?"

My tits and ass showed up just this summer, and I have the stretch marks to prove it. There's no way I'd feel comfortable swimming in anything besides one of my dad's XXL T-shirts. "Not bad," I say, leaning into her. "I like that snake-around-the-neck idea."

"DON'T MANGLE YOURSELF," IS what Bo would say when she'd catch me pulling at my lip, chewing on my cuticles. Or I'd be pushing my thumbs into my eyelids like I've done since I was a little girl, distracting myself from worry with pulsing shapes and sharp colors. But Bo fixed me. "Stop mashing your eyeballs," she'd say, swatting at my hands. I used to twist my lashes out, too, one by one, gentle and slow to keep the root intact. At the base of each hair there's this little wet bulb, a miniature globe you can crush with your teeth.

THE CASHIER COMES BACK with a box of witches, a tube of cream, a roll of gauze. "Let's get you cleaned up," he says, his hand out across the counter to take Bo's. There's a serious look on his acned face. It's control masked as concern, and it's sinister.

"Bless your precious heart," I say. Maybe you have to be from where we're from to know how a phrase like that can cut.

Bo lets his hand hang there, blinking away time with a slow bat of her lashes. I love it when she's like this, badass and stubborn, but a few more beats and even I want the whole thing to end. I study the reckless places where I've scraped off my nail polish, the shrinking continents left behind. Finally the cashier jerks his hand away, drops the stuff on the counter, and steps back, his ears hog pink. Then Bo says, "I said soft pack," to the poor bastard. "Not box."

He's suddenly intent on arranging a display of sunglasses. A woman takes over, tosses Bo's cigarettes on the counter without looking at us. "Together?" she asks. She rings up our snacks—more road food full of rainbow dye.

Bo knocks me with her hip. "We come from oil," she stage-whispers, her still-bleeding hand cupped around her mouth. "Famous family. You'd know our name if I said it." The lady doesn't look up from punching in prices.

"We're not related," I say.

"Fine," Bo says, and pouts. To the lady she says, "But we could be, though, right?"

"I LIKE HOW LINDA asks, 'Which time is it?'" I say. "She still say that?"

BO LEANS AGAINST AN ice cooler. She pours Mountain Dew over her gash and watches it fizz. I say, "Do you have any idea what that stuff is made of?"

She turns and gets a faceful of light. "There's glass in me," she says, cheerful, showing how the sun makes tiny shards glint through the neon froth. She wipes her hand on her shirt and loops gauze around her palm in a big, puffy glove. She tap-taps out a smoke for me. "Coffin nail?" she asks. "Witch for my bitch?" I can't get used to that word. If one of my brothers ever used it, my dad would get the bar of soap. My mom would cry. I try it out in text messages, where I can hide behind stupid spelling: *whats up bish? Howdy beeeotch!* I want to work it into conversation, but for now I can't bring myself to say the word aloud.

Bo knows I don't smoke. She takes the cigarette out with her teeth, slides the pack down into her cutoffs. I wonder where, exactly, it ends up. She makes a big show of striking a match, cupping the flame. Eyes closed, she shakes out the little fire, lets her jaw fall open. That first cloudy breath seeps free, then it's up, up, through her nose. I bet she's practiced in front of a mirror. Nicotine theater, she calls this whole bit.

BO TELLS ME HOW she and Linda still sit on the front porch together sometimes, take walks around the neighborhood with their arms linked. I took walks like that with Linda, too, a long time ago. She'd point to each object and say its name. "Mailbox," she would say, learning. "Dog bowl," and I'd say, "Exactly." Sometimes Linda asks Bo questions. "You like red color?" she'll say, and Bo, so happy there can be no wrong answer, will say, "Yes. Yes, I do."

BO SAYS, "BINGO," AND pulls over.

"Oh, Lord," I say.

She gets out of the car with me, but she stays put, leans against the hot hood. "Find us something good, Sister," she says. She's scrolling through her phone, checking to see if Jeff has texted. As I walk away I check my phone, too, probably for the same reasons Bo does: out of habit and guilt, because I miss his dumb face, because I still love everyone I've ever loved. Sometimes he sends us identical messages. Or worse, he'll try something out on one of us—a clever line, an anecdote—and then he'll revise the thing, improve upon it in some way, and send it to the other one. He doesn't realize yet that we're always together, that he's mostly what we talk about.

I'VE HAD ALMOST NO loss in my life, but I still believe we're always in between tragedies, that anything good is a lull before the next devastation. Somehow Bo blots out these fears, even the very legitimate dying that might happen as a result of this latest stupidity: on my phone is a picture of the mushroom strain we want, plus a picture of a poisonous, seemingly identical one. I've been leaning over stinking patties for weeks, finding nothing but flies, but today I see them: tan caps on thin stalks that bruise purple when you press on them. I flip one over; the gills are gray and powdery, the falling spores tinted navy, not black. *Psilocybe cubensis.*

I HAVE A MESSAGE from Jeff, just a *Hey*. Bo's probably got a *Hey you*, which is a very different kind of thing. If she responds and tells him I'm out scouring a pasture, he'll probably send me a *Hay there*. Poor, lonely Jeff.

HE TAUGHT ME HOW to twist out a tick so the head doesn't come off inside you.

———

I SHOULD BE PARANOID about cops driving by or some Cletus shooting me in the face for trespassing. I could get kicked by a cow, stung by a yellow jacket, fall into a well like that well-baby did. It looks like chain-saw psychos hang out here, haunted barns looming in the distance.

I WAS MOST AFRAID of getting lost. This was before my brothers were born, when it was just my mom and me in the supermarket. I'd hold a clutch of her skirt in my sweaty fist. I thought if I dropped it she'd be gone forever, or somehow *I'd* be gone forever. Eventually, in what I now realize was an act of kindness, she started wrenching herself free. "Close your eyes and stay here," she'd say. Time away from her was thick, slow and terrifying. "Okay," she'd call, and I'd open my eyes to see that she'd put a few paces between us. She'd wave at me. "See?" she'd say, down the aisle a little, off to the side, farther and farther, until one day she was just a voice, a phantom mother saying, "You're fine, Sara, see? You don't need me." But I did—and for a long time, too, much longer than either of us might have hoped.

BO SAYS EVERYTHING THAT scares you is something to poke at with a stick, to pick up and turn in your hands. Getting through it is the only way to get through it. I tell myself the caked-on cow shit is mud, then throw a clump of those suckers into my paper bag. Bo is seeping into me. Here I am, striding back to her. See how calm? How Bo-like in my grace?

THIS DOESN'T FEEL AS bad as I thought it would—it's less like drugs, more like vegetables. I put the paper bag in the cup holder, like a snack. "Gimme," Bo says, and takes a peek. "They're so cute!" she says. "These are totally the right ones. I'm like fifty percent sure." Her blood smears on the brown paper.

"Your bandage is full," I say.

"Who cares!" she says. "What a day!" She eyeballs an appropriate serving size, makes us choke down the same amount at the same time. We chase them with Skittles, but there's mash left in my molars, an aftertaste like dirty peanut shells. "Done," Bo says. "Now we won't trip or die alone. It's win-win."

"MAYBE LINDA'S ONLY SWEET in English," Bo says, "but I don't want to know." She reaches over and blindly grabs the soda from my lap. She shakes the ice around, takes a long pull. My thighs are cold where the drink was—the skin feels like someone else's. My pockets hang below the hem of my cut-offs where I let Bo slash them too short. "Bonnie couldn't get pregnant the normal way," Bo says. "She had a doctor mix me up in a dish."

I say, "So that's why she couldn't afford braces. She spent every penny sciencing you to life."

Bo says, "But she's about as maternal as one of those real big lizards." I'm quiet then, sorting through reptiles in my mind. The road is getting crunchier, the farmhouses farther apart. I'm thinking monitor lizard. I'm thinking Komodo dragon, or are those the same deal? Not loving, is Bo's point. Not like Linda.

I TELL BO THAT my stomach hurts, that my bowels are roiling. "Same!" she says, excited. "It's coming."

"Can you drive on these?" I ask.

"Probably!" Bo says.

"CAN YOU IMAGINE DAVID and Linda giving up gene splicing or whatever it was they did?" Bo says. "Just so their kids could be American?"

"Jeff got *too* American," I say. Bo says there's still hope for Candy. "Candy's worse!" I say. I tell Bo how she used to steal money from Linda's purse, how she was always falling into these quiet, calculated rages. "One time a neighborhood kid called her a cunt. She broke into his garage and took his bicycle apart piece by piece. She spread the guts out in perfect rows on his driveway! Candy's disturbed," I say.

"Yeah," Bo says, "she's shady, but she plays the violin and she's studying to be an engineer, so . . ."

I can't believe Bo just said that. "I can't believe you just said that," I say.

"What, that she's doing the dutiful Chinese bit?" Bo says. "It's true—Jeff agrees! And even if it's just on paper, Linda and David will eat it up, and the world will, too."

WE PASS YET ANOTHER vasectomy-reversal billboard, this one of a gummy, drooling baby with a bow stuck on its head, a cartoon bubble at the top that says, "No scalpels! No needles!"

"I don't even get it," I say. "That's supposed to be, what? Something the baby's saying to try and get born?"

BO USED TO MAKE Jeff translate Linda's ghost stories, one sentence at a time. "They have real ghosts over there," Bo says. The three of them would sit in the kitchen, Bo tapping her foot under the table, waiting in protracted terror for the story to come through Jeff.

"Or maybe it's what that baby is thinking," Bo says. In her spooky voice she says, "From beyond the beyond." She says it a few more times, in different tones at different speeds. Or does she? "Sip," Bo says, and smacks her lips open. My depth perception is a hair off—I have a hard time not poking her in the face with the straw.

———

THIS IS THE SECOND-BEST Linda story, according to Bo: When Linda was a young girl, she waited tables at her father's fancy, haunted restaurant. "One night, when everyone else had gone home, Linda saw a woman sleeping on a couch in the powder room, a book spread open on her face." The car thump-thumps on the shoulder until Bo brings us back into our lane.

"I don't want to have psychedelic diarrhea," I whine.

Bo snorts and says, "We take the trip we need to take."

I USED TO THINK I could learn by listening alone. Jeff's parents would call him into the living room, and I'd eavesdrop from the table, over the vast spread of our books and papers. They talked too fast, nonsense shot through with words like "Walmart" or "Honda," sometimes even my name. I often worried that he was in trouble because of the volume and tone his parents used with him. "What happened?" I'd say, nervous, when he returned to the kitchen. "They wanted directions to the car wash," he'd say, something innocuous like that.

"IT WASN'T TOTALLY UNCOMMON to see a person reclining like this, but it was after hours and the woman was completely asleep. Linda had to watch for the rise and fall of her chest, to make sure the woman was breathing. So she's telling me this story in this low voice," Bo says. "Sometimes she's imitating the sleeping woman, breaking in with her sweet little hand gestures. Bit by bit, the story came through Jeff. Waiting for it made me want it more, and I was getting so freaked out." Bo rides right up on a semitruck's ass. Gravel and dust spray the windshield. She floors it, gives the driver the bird and a big smile as we fly by.

"LINDA NEEDS TO WAKE this lady up, so she clears her throat and says, 'Excuse me, miss,' or whatever the expression is over there, but the woman doesn't move. Linda gets closer and closer, repeating herself. Still the woman won't move. Linda's close enough now that she can see the book covering the woman's face. The title didn't translate. It made no sense, not even to Linda. It was like, word salad, just freaky nothing. Finally, she leans over and puts her hand on the lady's shoulder. By now I was terrified, squeezing Jeff's arm. Linda was gesturing at her face, her fingers streaming down. I asked, 'What is she saying?' I'm like, 'Oh my God, *Jeff*, what did she see?'"

UP AHEAD WE SEE that an eighteen-wheeler has somehow crashed itself, spilled Day-Glo sludge all over the highway. We haven't come across another car for miles, but everybody is clumped up here, flares burning orange around the wreckage. Traffic crawls. "Oh no," I say, "it's people." I think maybe I am starting to feel something beyond the beyond.

———

THERE WAS A FRACTURE in the second-best ghost story. Jeff couldn't say what Linda saw, not right away. "She just closed her eyes and kept moving her fingers fast down her face. And Jeff was kind of annoyed by everything, frustrated, like always, that I wanted to hang out with his mom. He's all, 'She's saying there was just more hair, like the back of a woman's head but on the front.' Like hair went *all the way around*." Bo looks to me for a reaction, and I think of how a human face works, all the muscles that have to get together to form an expression. She says, "It gave me chills. I was shuddering. And Linda just looked at me and in English she said, 'Hair face,'" Bo says. "She was really pleased with herself."

"YOU'LL LIKE THIS," BO says. She keeps her eyes on the road but tugs her tank top up, shows me a curved pink scar on her rib. "Childhood bite," she says.

"Big lizard?" I say.

"Ha," she says. "Human day care kid." Bo's bra is purple mesh with a single flimsy clasp, the whole thing more for show than support. Her foot is off the gas, and we're drifting around, straddling both lanes. This is fine with me, somehow.

"Broke the skin," I say. I trace my thumb over the raised shape.

"Yep," she says. Her skin pimples up. "And then I broke

that little shit's face." I add the bite to the tally of marks she's already shown me: there's chicken pox, a fishhook, a tiny silver dot from a number two pencil. I've filed these details away, tucked them into the hot folds of my brain. It's cruel, really, what she can do to me.

JEFF KISSED ME ONCE, when we were thirteen. I'd just beaten him at some video game—obliterated his high score—and I thought he was mad until he lunged, openmouthed, and hugged me with his whole body. I memorized the shape of that moment, and then I pulled away. I laughed and laughed. He showed me what I was, without meaning to. He was all fat tongue and dumb want, his dick like a dog in the room, begging for attention.

BO IS OUT OF injuries, out of birthmarks and moles, too. She drives with one leg hiked up on the seat, her shirt tucked into her bra, her bandaged hand curled into her bare stomach. It's an act, right? All of it. It's an act, but it's an act I can believe in. Every thought feels profound and true, even conflicting thoughts. I hate my mother, and it's true. I love my mother, and it's true. Bo is needy and horrible, and I am needy and horrible, and Jeff is needy and horrible. Linda is still the best. Bo looks straight ahead at the road, and I look at her. "I know about silos," she says, no silo in sight.

———

OR NO, IT'S REAL, all of it.

I YAWN, AND IT'S my face opening up in a big way. "Stop it," Bo says. "That shit's contagious." And it's true—the spasm jumps from my face to hers. It's a thrill to watch. "God-almighty-damn," she says, mouth open wide, voice so loud. It's true that her back teeth are all done up in dull metallic. She lights a cigarette in a microversion of the smoke show, and we finally creep up right next to the jackknifed truck, the flares and flashing lights. She beeps out a little rhythm on the horn with her bum hand, waves at the hazmat crew. "This is so much fun," she says as we sluice through the bright mess.

"DID HE SHOW YOU those pictures of him in that crotchless baby outfit?" I ask Bo.

"What?" she says, turning her head hard and fast, side to side, to shake out what I've said. "No! And let's never say those words together in a sentence."

There is some kind of golden fur on Bo, on everything I look at, really. I can see these rainbow hairs all over her clothes, too, like she's been wrestling iridescent cats. The car is full of textures—what's clean is dirty, what's dirty is filthy. I check out a crumpled burger wrapper by my foot. It's not moving, but it seems alive, and friendly, too.

I say, "Linda and David pointed them out to me in the

family album. It's this really normal thing they do, they're so proud to show off that the baby is a boy. They get them in these crotchless outfits so everyone can see the little baby dick. Not all the time, obviously—that would be creepy. Only in family pictures."

Bo says, "Yeah, that doesn't sound creepy at all."

"Gotta celebrate the boy babies," I say.

BO IS PULLING OVER, but the road is a tongue slurping us to the side. The tongue is dry and black, like a parrot's. It's getting dark, or maybe it's that there's too much stuff floating in the air, blocking out the sun. Outside it's empty and dusty and brown, and Jesus, do I love Texas. "I'm so annoyed right now," Bo says. The hollows under her cheeks are big holes, kind of breathing. "Where's Candy's crotchless baby outfit? What the shit is that about?"

I CAN'T TELL HOW much of this is mushrooms and how much of it is just being in a car bubble with Bo. I'm very aware that we are organisms on the surface of a rock, orbiting a burning star. Bo has her shirt off, and she's looking down at herself, saying, "If this is what I look like, then I'm okay with it."

I say, "You aren't usually okay with how you look?"

And she says, "No. No, I'm not."

This shocks me, how someone like Bo could feel anything but celestial. She's wiggled out of her gauze glove. We're in the back. I keep thinking the headrest on the driver's seat is a person's head. It's Linda shaped. "She's a great chauffeur," I say, and Bo knows exactly what I mean.

WE'RE CLOSE TOGETHER AND my shirt is off, too, so our lungs can feel each other, we say. This is chaste. We're children finding the edges of our bodies, trying to fit everything in our mouths. She's reopened the cut in her hand, and it's bleeding again, blood on my face, my tits, blurring the car windows. "Shouldn't this be scary?" we ask, the back seat like a massacre, but it's not, not at all. My eyes are having trouble keeping track, and there's my nose in between them, ruining everything. Bo says Jeff's dad taught her to do eye exercises. David says that the eye muscles are the most overlooked, that they need to be maintained like anything else. "Can we just stop with Jeff's family for a little bit?" I say. "Can we just say there is a jar for Jeff and a jar for Candy and a jar for David and a jar for Linda? Can we do that, please?"

AND WE DO—WE PUT them all in jars.

"SEE," BO SAYS. "THIS is the place. This is us, better." And it's true. "Aw," Bo says, "I like Jeff so much." She's looking over in the general vicinity of Jeff's jar, Jeff sitting calm and sweet inside. For the first time I'm not at all threatened by this. I'm not sad, either. Jeff will forgive me, maybe he already has. I like Jeff, too, so much. Jeff's the best. "Can we?" Bo asks. We take Linda out of her jar, just for a little while.

ONCE A YEAR, THE dead moved through the little town where Linda grew up. All the young men killed at war would be called up at once to make their way to the Yellow River, where they would turn into herons and fly away. They flooded the streets at dusk, they looked straight ahead and made their long way to the water. The dead looked just like us, Linda said, only lurching and silent, with white bandages wrapped around their wounds. These dead boys rode the bus together, walked the streets, did everything the living do, but if you tried to engage them, they would fall to the ground. Then you'd have a corpse, not a heron, and this was very bad luck. As a precaution, a runner came hours before the dead did, to warn the townspeople that this slow parade was coming. Women and children were kept inside, but one year, Linda begged her parents to let her stay up. There was no way to keep death a secret forever, so they decided she might as well see it for herself. After the runner came through, hoarse from screaming, his clothes heavy with jangling bells, Linda's father made a loop for her foot with his hands and hoisted her up to the window. Her story stops here. She slowly shook her head. She couldn't put into words what she saw, but we can imagine it: the thrust of the broken, staggering bodies. How it must have looked when those dead boys finally touched their toes to the water, fell to their knees, and burst into birds.

WE'RE COMING DOWN. "FAST," I say.

Bo says, "We took it easy on you."

Objects are still cheerful—the gearshift, the sun visors—but there is a calm, sober heart at the center of everything. Bo kisses me, and it's wintergreen. We aren't children playing games. Linda isn't driving the car anymore. It's just us, two girls alone in the back seat, wearing some of each other's clothes.

BO STRADDLES ME, AND it's bliss. "Am I crushing you?" she asks.

"Not at all," I say.

"I feel like you're smaller than me," she says. "If you want to switch."

"Only if you want to," I say. "But you're definitely smaller."

"Maybe we're samesies," she says. We move together in the dark car. "Shall we commence the procedure?" Bo whispers. It's a joke, but it's true that neither of us is exactly sure how to harness what we have.

I'M WORKING BO WITH my hands. This goes on in such a way that I can leave and come back to it. I take breaks, visit my childhood bedroom in my mind, sit in a comfy chair in my dead grandmother's knocked-down house. Helping Bo is a noble and difficult task, like trying to jerk off a beam of light. When she's finished with my hand, she shifts her body up, and I shift my body down and her panties go to the side. My panties. She hates the word "panties." We both do. We stop what we're doing to think of an alternative. "Undies?" we try.

"Intimates?" I offer.

"Ugh," she says. "Intimates is so much worse."

I'm thinking intimates anyway—I can't control it. I pull Bo's intimates, my intimates, to the side. I'm going to tell her this later, to annoy her. But now it's puzzle time, serious. I'm going to figure her out.

"I take forever," Bo says.

And I say, "I like forever," only I say it kind of into her body, like a secret, and I don't know if she hears. There's no better place to be than this—on the cusp, aching at the start of something. There's no performance happening, just a figure saying what it wants, another figure answering. It's the kind of sex so good you want it to hurry up and be over so you can talk about it for the rest of your life. Or it's not, but that's something I think of while I'm having it, some way I might describe it later. She's showing me shortcuts, and she's right, she does take forever—it's taking forever to get her off. But now that she's getting close, now I don't want it to end.

THE ANIMAL PART

CIMARRON JIM IS JUST SOMEBODY somebody else made up. He's to keep campers from wrecking the woods. If you're a litterbug, if you ruin baby birds with your human smell and they starve, if you don't douse your finished campfires to death, Cimarron Jim takes note, strike one. Strike two is a red bandanna tied to your tent. Strike three is unspeakable, Giddy says.

Giddy is out there in the flashlit midnight, flicking snails into my splayed sleeping bag. At first I don't know that it's Giddy doing the flicking and that what he's flicking are snails. When things are small and round and sailing into your open tent hole, falling on your pillow and pegging your canteen, what you think is: rocks. It isn't until I catch one midflight and feel the perfect spiral that I know.

I'm never asleep. I've tried the tricks, listed state capitals and alphabetized all the girls in my class I want to
kiss, counted pretend animals and breaths and heartbeats.
I've imagined my brain waves swiped off a chalkboard by a
pretty teacher's naked forearm. I try to have no thoughts or
the thoughts of a monk or a roasted marshmallow or a dead
kid, but it's no use in my bed at home, let alone woods like
these.

Another snail skitters, and then that little voice calls from
the bosky dark. He's trying to sound ghostly, but the type
of voice Giddy has already, up high and bratty like that, I
don't know, maybe it's just a style of voice that's too hard to
get around. Giddy, or the shape I take for Giddy, tells me
he's got an idea for a trap.

"If this Jim has feet—if he walks on land—then we can't
go wrong," he squeaks.

He wants to scoop out a hole, fill it with leaves so it reads
like flatland. "We'll take turns," he says, breathless. "We'll
co-scoop."

He wants to bait the pit, put his best around the edges.
"Creature comforts," he says: his breezer hat with the chin
strap, his dead dad's compass with the studded gem above
the N, a whole thing of water purification tablets. He wants
me to sweeten the pot with some insect repellent. Never
mind that Cimarron Jim is at worst the ghost of a skinned
Indian wandering the woods for all eternity, at best a rogue
forest ranger waiting to touch our dicks.

"Every woodsman has needs," Giddy says in that stupid
voice. "Deep needs."

When it isn't summer we aren't friends. Giddy has a bunch of big brothers who are noisy and tough and don't trust anyone who isn't blood. They go anywhere they please in our neighborhood—to find them, just look for the pile of bikes. They have a mom who can't stand up without a kid under each armpit. She breathes from a tank and is so sick when you look at her you get that creepy feeling like when you see a picture of Earth from outer space.

The plan is to sleep in the trees, Giddy says, wait for our moment. He says the animal part of us won't let us fall.

I say, "Jesus, Giddy, you are one dumb shit," but okay, fine. It's kid stuff, but what else have I got going on?

I'm lying still for a second, shaking out this weird black thought I was having about one of those underwater sea cows, something boat scarred and smart that barely breathes. I'm not pulling on my pants or making a me-shaped lump in the sleeping bag in case a counselor comes looking—not yet. I'm not smearing my face with mud like I bet Giddy has done, not yet zipping my black hoodie all the way up, delinquent style. But I'm split already into the me who is here sleepless and lonely and the me who is outside, tearing through the cicada-choked dark with Giddy, gasping.

FOXES

WHAT'S WORTH HAPPENING HAPPENS IN deep woods. Or so my daughter tells me.

Her plotlines: In the deep woods someone is chasing, someone else is getting hacked. Hatchets are lifted, brought downdowndown. Men stutter blood onto snow. A cast of animals—some local, some outlandish—show up to feast on the bits. "The bitty bits," she'll say, "the tasty remainderings." Good luck diverting her. Good luck correcting or getting a word in once she gets going. It's gruesome, but this type of storytelling, I've been assured, is perfectly normal among children her age.

I have a fat stack of books concerned with the inner lives of little girls. I have glossy pamphlets, full-color articles

I've taken from waiting rooms. Her stories may be distasteful, but my daughter is happiest describing dark-spattered worlds. Routine is what's important, all the experts agree. Stability. So tonight is the same. "Woods it is," I say when she takes me by the wrist.

I'm the first to admit it—I tune her out. I know there are foxes in her stories—I know there are men. She misses the dogs, maybe. She misses her father. She's an excitable kid, prone to rushed speech. Truthfully, she spits. I'm told this mess is evidence of a rich mind. Doctors say it, teachers. My girl has strands of dazzling beads hidden in that throat. She pulls them up from somewhere rich, way in the back.

The tent she's fashioned is small and drab, a sagging thing posted by a pair of barstools. Soiled, pulled straight from our beds, these drooping sheets are my daughter and myself layered, fitted and flat. She scurries inside, whistles for me.

I bunch up and crawl through, hem in hand, nude hose flashing, nude pumps kicked off. The air inside is damp, trapped and sharp from her socked feet. My cheap and not cheap perfumes mix and float.

I'm taking too long to settle. My daughter's big, wet eyes are over there in the dark where I can't see them, rolling at me while I struggle. My friction drags dust and old fur up from the carpet. I've been meaning to vacuum, but the machine is in the upstairs closet, heavy with a full bag, a whole skein of orange yarn caught around one of the bristles.

My daughter sighs. "Patience is a muscle," I remind her. Hers is puny, a weak slick of lavender. My knees don't bend how they used to. My head is doming the roof.

Her flashlight clicks on, catches a universe of grit and leftover dog. There's Bit-Bit and Rowdy and Poco turning in the air. Specks of my daughter and me, of my fool ex-husband. Our old family, filthy and granular.

"Ready?" she says.

DEEP IN THE WOODS, the knight is running.

"From whom?" I ask my daughter.

"From let me tell it," she says.

SHE'S NOT GOING TO like it, but I've forgotten something crucial, an important part of our routine.

"Half a second," I say.

I reverse scoot, wreck against a barstool, threaten the entire design. My daughter hisses. "Bass ackward" is what the fool would call this maneuver, and he wouldn't be wrong.

I'm quick at the wet bar. A dirty glass is pretty clean when you're the only one who uses it, when you enjoy the same drink every time. There's scarlet lipstick gobbed on the rim, all me.

I get back in the tent before my daughter's feelings are hurt. Her light catches cut crystal in my hand, scatters blue and yellow sparks. "Sherry," I say. It doesn't need to be said, but I like the word. A secretary's drink, a middle-class nightcap. She knows I'm finished forever with the red-topped bottles and the black-topped bottles, the plastic bottles with tops I lost, bottles that left clear sludge in every coffee mug in this house.

My daughter beams my face like a cop. I take a sip, dainty, then lift the sheet, break the seal. I push my drink under, outside but not away. This is me being responsible. I tuck myself in at the wrist, a cold hand out to touch the beaded glass. Just sherry!

"By all means," I tell her. "Go on."

My daughter's teeth are gray with white flecks. When she tells, foam gathers in her corners, drips in ribbons under her chin. She spews. My only job is not to flinch.

Flashlit, she looks nothing like me.

DEEP IN THE WOODS, the knight is running. He will do whatever it takes to get back home.

HER TEETH ARE MY fault. Weak dentin on my side of the tree—our photo albums are full of snarled smiles. Gum disease going back through the ages. White sores and also clicky jaws, people predisposed to clench and do damage even as they slept. Plus, my daughter's precious grape soda is corrosive, I'm told. I push water and milk, but she fights me.

She may not be pretty, but my girl's brain is just fine.

It is. She dodged the worst genes, somehow. Her father, the fool, was a man who broke the binding of *The Biggest Ever Book of Party Jokes,* kept the glue-crusted pages paper-clipped or rubber-banded, dog-eared in his glove compartment, crammed into his blue jeans.

The fool said, "What's black and white and . . . wait. Wait."

Then fumbling, dull flipping.

I'm not much better. At my daughter's age I folded my failures into textbooks, blamed broken chalk for my public mistakes. Even now I count the months on my knuckles and navigate the world by making an L out of one hand.

"I've got country smarts," the fool used to say, his arm deep in some majestic carcass he'd tracked for days and shot for fun.

It's not the fault of the deplorable towns where the fool and I grew up—him in the bleak piney woods near the penitentiary, me up where Texas bludgeons Oklahoma, in a county known for making glue. Both of us were jaundiced preemies. Both of us were nursed on evaporated milk instead of formula, sucked on toys coated with lead paint. Whether it's nature or nurture, for people like the fool and me there is a long beat between learning something and knowing it. For us, answers come later, when we're far away from the question, if they come at all.

He makes money, lots of it, which obscures his deficiencies. I overcompensate, read what I can, take expert advice.

At least I know what I don't know, which is more than I can say for the fool.

DEEP IN THE WOODS, the knight is running. He will do whatever it takes to get back to his family. The woods are full of enemies—hooded men setting traps, wearing black cloaks. Men with needle-nose pliers. But the knight is unstoppable. He has been on the move for so long. He has leaped out of snares, set fire to cloaked men. He has turned pliers around on the bad guys, ripped their eyelids off in self-defense.

I'M NOT SURE HOW my daughter managed it, but in this altogether different deplorable town—awful for nicer reasons: spring breakers and prefab houses, eggy-smelling tap water—she is the best and brightest in her young class. I've got a bumper sticker that says, "Ask me about my honors student." She comes home with her backpack full of flash cards, arms cuffed in rolled-up poster board. She taught the dogs—when we still had the dogs—to sit in Spanish.

"Eureka!" she shrieks, three, four times a night.

This house is nothing like the mobile homes the fool and I grew up in, full of boilerplate poverty and the lazy rage that comes with it. Me fighting my sisters for stolen ketchup packets, the fool dunking his dingy little brothers in week-old bathwater.

My girl has a writing desk and an electric pencil sharpener. She lists endangered species over alphabet soup, says she will be an architect and a veterinarian and an astronaut and a mommy. Shampoo horned, she sings a song of South American capitals, sketches the water cycle on a steamy shower door. When I'm toweling her off, I trace cursive letters on her back—sweet little notes just for her. No matter how fast I spell them out, she never misses a word.

Through those teeth, my daughter tells me about baobab trees.

"Have you heard of our ecosystem?" she asks when I tuck her in. "Have you heard of my inner beauty and my outer beauty?"

DEEP IN THE WOODS, the knight is lost. He has been hunted for so long, running and running, but he has not come to the edge of the woods in all this time. He worries that he has been going in circles or in the wrong direction. The knight will do whatever it takes to get back to his child, but he needs a new plan. He knows he must leave some sign of himself behind.

"Can I borrow bread crumbs?" my daughter asks. "From the one with those kids and the oven witch?"

"Of course," I say, thrilled to see her comprehension and recall at work. "Take whatever you need."

I don't dare check it now, but outside the tent, my drink is almost empty. You can tell by the temperature of the glass.

The knight leaves a trail: focaccia and croutons, big hunks of Wonder Bread.

"Fairy-tale bullcrap," her father would say, were he here.

The fool believed himself to be a master of deep woods. "In real life," he'd say, "people bend branches to show where they've been."

THERE'S NO ACCOUNTING FOR charisma—the fool was a man's man and a ladies' man, too. Silver fox, sly dog. He wore full-quill ostrich boots, glided his starched Mexican wedding shirt skinnyways through the room. His quick smile propped up dimples stitched deep in rawhide. A big tipper, a Southern gent. He was good in bars, good in places that muffled him. Those terrible jokes: the Helen Kellers and the knock-knocks, so many stupid blondes.

The fool and I argued. We were most brutal in cars, coming from or heading toward the next humiliation. We fought about women and we fought about men. At parties, I talked small with strangers and double-fisted drinks before I went looking. I'd find the fool in a dark room, his face caught by the light from a refrigerator door, a passing car. The partygoer or hostess turning, buttoning, zipping.

"Honeybaby," he'd say to me, cornered. "Where have you been all my life?"

"Take me drunk, I'm home," went the fool, on his knees in the coatroom, belly-up in the bushes when I went for the car.

He was much older, with a fortune coming, an oil well he dangled when I pretend-packed my bags or sat crying on a suitcase. By then there was the daughter, diapered and snapped, gummy and drooling, strapped into a car seat out in the hall. I was twenty-three with a cesarean scar and a court-reporting certificate. The fool paid our mortgage, had a trust fund for his only child. I wasn't going anywhere.

"Come back, baby. Baby, please come back," he crooned.

One weekend the fool went on a bender and smashed every light in this house. I spent my Sunday screwing in bulbs.

"Hey!" the fool said from our bed, still drunk. "How many yous does it take?"

DEEP IN THE WOODS, the bread crumbs aren't really working.

THE FOOL SAID HE was sweating like a whore in church. Could I open a window now and again? He was so hungry he could eat the crotch out of a rag doll, suck the cunt from a low-flying duck. Would it kill me to pop him a cold beer? How about cracking an egg for a change?

The fool was no saint, and I was no homemaker. We could have afforded a housekeeper, a personal chef. But the fool wanted me to hone my skills. I drank to keep up, but I was no drinker, not yet. My talent was sleeping it off. I brought hangover cures into bed with me: ginger ale with a splash of Tabasco and an effervescent tablet, the glass seething on the bedside table. Mice showed up, chewed holes through the sleeves of my saltines, left droppings on the silk pillowcases, my marble vanity. Loose gems, I told myself. Black pearls. I wore a sleep mask and didn't mind. I dozed until three, hobbled to a lawn chair I'd transplanted in the shower. I was a lightweight, a pretty young thing, dressed to the nines by the time the fool came home.

He'd walk through the door, hungry after hunting. He'd say, "Sister, this broom ain't gonna push itself."

DEEP IN THE WOODS, the animals are helping. The knight whistles, and out they come: hordes of bears and birds and rabbits and foxes, all ready to assist him.

My daughter stops her story for fox facts. Did I know that foxes hunt alone? That they walk on their toes? I use this opportunity to answer her cheerfully as I slip out of the tent, like I have heard my phone buzz, like I have some small, pressing task. I do know about foxes, though I encourage her to continue with her list. I'm the one who selected *Everything Fox: A Children's Guide* from the library. I'm the one who has been reading it to her.

I'm back under the sheets right away.

"The knight," I say, chipper. I'm checking her face to see if the bottle registers. I've put it next to me like a pet.

With the animals' help, the knight knows he is heading in the right direction, but people keep getting in his way. Now he has his knee on somebody's throat, is cutting out somebody's floppy, purple tongue. He is feeding that tongue to a fox.

Did I know a fox can hear a man's watch ticking forty yards away? That foxes don't shiver? That a group of foxes is called a skulk?

Someone else is coming down the dark, wooded path. The knight is so brave and strong. He will kill the whole world to get back to his daughter.

Of course he will.

THE FOOL PICKED OUT the dogs, but our daughter gave them names. Two of them were rangy and energetic, hot-nosed breeds that could be trained on any scent. The other one was squat with soft ears, a short snout for mouthing dead birds. The fool would go away with this pack for weeks at a time, return with a truck bed full of bloody fur or feathers, depending on the season.

Even as a tiny thing, my daughter never seemed to mind slaughter. The fool would sit her on the workbench in the garage while he hacked and sawed, talked about his deep respect for the natural world.

I kept the dogs indoors after he left, because that's where they'd always been and because the child psychologist told me to. My daughter insisted she'd take full responsibility, but of course I ended up doing everything—filling the food and water bowls, putting flea drops between shoulder blades, hiding heartworm pills in hunks of cheese. For a time, I tried to pretend they were my dogs. I didn't mind the two trackers—they barked at solicitors and slept near my daughter's bed—but the tender-mouthed one was a real problem. He'd shit in the kitchen and claw at the hardwood. He'd roam the halls at night, whining for the fool.

I TOLD SOME LIES. What I said was: Your father loves you to bits. Your father is busy, but he is always thinking of you. Your father would visit, but he is living on the other side of the world. He would call, but he is in another time zone, is in a place with poor reception, has lost and broken his phone, has had it stolen. There's no mail over there, no stamps to buy, nothing coming in or out. Bit-Bit and Rowdy and Poco went to live in the country. You are sweet and smart and definitely not extremely strange. You are lovable and deserving of love—everybody is.

WHEN IT'S DEEP IN the woods and the knight stabs another man in the lung with a pencil just because and the air seeps out in an e-e-eeek, "Is there any better sound?" my daughter wants to know.

I POUR MYSELF A very reasonable pour.

I know about the stepped-on cracker in the dining room, the clots of mud around little shoes in the front hall. Of course I do! Those messes aren't new—I notice them every day, several times a day. But then I flash on the full vacuum bag, the upstairs closet. How heavy. The bristles, the orange skein. Children can't see grime—I read that, that they don't recognize dirt as separate from the thing that is dirty—so why bother?

IN THE DEEPEST, DARKEST woods, the knight cuts out a man's liver and tosses it to a fox. He cuts off two ears. Fox. Fox. He rips out a larnix as a snack for a wolf. Two larnixes!

"I believe it's pronounced *larynx*," I say gently, refilling my glass.

WITH NOTHING TO HUNT, the dogs became carpet barges, fat and begging for food. They stank and were noisy, and my daughter had lost interest in them, or seemed to, so I kept them locked in the laundry room. They were rambunctious and too much trouble to walk, so I'd take them outside one by one, straight to a tree and back. They dozed on big pillows, whined, and scratched. On rare occasions when I encouraged my daughter to play with them in our small enclosed garden—and she had to be forcefully encouraged, every time—they would run like crazy, knocking into one another and her, clawing into the dirt with their too-long nails, a frenzy of ecstatic barking. My daughter would soon get bored and want to come back inside, but it was nearly impossible for her to get a handle on the dogs. They'd evade and dodge, frothy tongues out, smiling the way dogs smile. Eventually I'd be tasked with wrangling them, jerking their choke chains, dragging them back to their dark cell.

———

DEEP IN THE WOODS, the knight is fashioning an ornament for his friends, the animals, one he will mount like a star to the highest tree. It will be made from the severed hands of his enemies. This is no easy task, my daughter says. She pantomimes the dissection, grunts to demonstrate the effort. It seems to me the knight is misusing his time, that he could stop with the disgusting detours if he's in such a rush to get back to his kid.

A twig snaps. Someone is coming down the dark, wooded path. It is yet another man, cloaked, carrying a piece of razor wire. Maybe you can guess where my daughter is headed with this.

The hooded man is a zombie, she says, no friend at all.

"Zombie why?" I say. "How?"

Annoyed, she informs me that these are new characters, that her plot has twisted.

"What about his daughter?" I ask, pouring myself a lovely pour. "You've left a lot of holes."

The knight and the zombie fight in a heap like dogs— storybook dogs that spin around and around until they turn to butter. I read her that one! But these two do not turn into butter. They blend and melt together until they are indistinguishable, until one dizzy cowboy is all that is left, naked, bleeding out at the base of a tree.

"Isn't that a little sloppy?" I say.

Things have changed since I last freshened my drink. My girl's stories are stories only in the loosest sense.

"The knight is no longer present?" I need clarification.

She glares, goes on, gives another butchered hand to the animals. Safety scissors are involved, the webbing between dead fingers must be sliced for some reason. I don't always need to follow her logic. The cutting is the point. The ripping apart.

DING-DONG IS WHAT THE fool called our daughter. Dingus.

"Whatcha doing, Ding-a-ling?" he would ask.

But what a genius the girl was even then, rolling over, sitting up, pulling herself to stand by our pant legs, propelling herself around the coffee table. There was no real tether between the two of them, my girl's glories wasted and unnoticed.

She doesn't need him now, either. She's well on her way to growing up, becoming a real person. She has preferences she has come to on her own. Sophisticated tastes. For example, she is crazy for artichoke hearts and capers. Capers!

There are tricks to coping with a surly person you've brought into the world. Focus on the positive. Maintain a cheery outlook, relish small personal pleasures.

Because of the teeth, my daughter looks like she has been drinking red wine. I swear she hasn't!

"ARE YOU BLACKED OUT now?" the fool wanted to know. "How about now?"

It was one of his jokes, one of his insults. I could match

him shot for shot, but not without consequence. Lost keys, broken ribs, a cue ball I tried to bite like an apple.

"Did I have fun?" I had to ask him.

Did I?

Then the girl was born, and things changed not at all. We went about our business with babysitters. Beths and Bonnies. Never a Tanya, never a risk like a Stacy. I liked my girls acned, fluorescent rubber bands stretching at the backs of their mouths.

"You are a motherfucker," I slurred at the fool as a hand-wringing Beth looked on from the couch, some horrified Bonnie waited for her ride.

"You are nouveau riche—trash with cash." I fed the fool his greatest fear.

This after a sickening discovery: photos of some mixed-up kid, an unseemly queen posed in purple panties and the fool's ten-gallon hat.

"What does that make you?" the fool shot back. "You, without a pot of your own to piss in?"

Or maybe I didn't really say those things, not out loud. Maybe this time there was not a Beth or a Bonnie present. It was only the fool on the couch, on his back, boots in the air. A bag of peas on his face to soothe the eyeball I scratched with a tossed Polaroid. Maybe the girl was not yet born. It is possible I am remembering things in the wrong order or remembering them out of scale.

The last straw had nothing to do with one of the fool's women or one of the fool's men. It had to do with me, of all people, and something small that I did, stretched out of proportion in the fool's fool mind.

IT MAKES NO DIFFERENCE to the fool that my daughter is on the honor roll. He doesn't care that she's reading above grade level, that she's scoring off the charts in math. For all he knows, she's the oldest in her young class. There is no water cycle, there are no South American capitals. It's not his problem that she tells horrifically violent, psychologist-approved stories. He doesn't mind when she makes ridiculous demands, when she is entitled and nasty, in the throes of some demonic tantrum. For all he knows, she has regressed steadily backward since he went away. Maybe she babbles now, gurgles like someone born without a tongue, someone who has never learned to speak.

IN THE DEEP WOODS, not all the animals are so nice. Don't forget there are panthers hiding out here. They are skinny and pissed off. They are coiled in the trees like furry, pissed-off springs, ready.

It occurs to me to be more careful about the language I use around the child. Mimicry, though—it's akin to intelligence, is it not?

She's mad at me because I've spilled, drenched my sherry hand, gotten the carpet wet. I'll clean it up later, with all the rest of it. I'll take the kitchen scissors upstairs to the vacuum cleaner and cut the yarn, do that part, at least. I've decided that will be my first step, should I choose to take it.

DEEP IN THE WOODS, blah, blah, blah. My manners are the first thing to go. I try to keep tabs, but I am never drinking from a can. I keep track in my own way. Am I blinking regularly? Can I feel my mouth? Sherry is a pretty drink that warms up the light around your face. No harm can come, I remind my daughter.

The trick to paying attention is nodding at intervals, occasional squinting, a rutted brow. Children are the easiest. They do not care that you are listening—only that they are speaking.

My daughter's teachers used to ask me to decode her. Muchbah was lunchbox, creen was crayon. There was pock-pock, goo. A mother should know.

"We have such a tough time," they would say. "Nothing but garble from this one here."

ABOUT THE LAST STRAW: It's true that I dropped dirty diapers out of the window and down into the bushes over a brief period of weeks. It wasn't as if I dropped them onto the front lawn, and at least I wasn't leaving our daughter to stink in some corner of her crib. They landed on the side of the house, out of sight from the street. Obviously, I intended to retrieve the mess at a later date, but the fool took my pile personally, called it a "grisly discovery," said it was "proof of a real problem."

Perhaps the fool broke only one light bulb, or perhaps I broke it myself. Perhaps the bulb burned out on its own, or I changed it before it had a chance to pop.

DEEP IN THE WOODS, the cowboy must defeat the final enemy, an inky shape that has been looming this whole time, ruining everything, chasing him away. The shape descends from the dark sky, retching and twisting, singing a terrible song. She brings her inky face close to the cowboy's face. Her eyes are black, sparkly disks. Her teeth are really pointy. She smells like somebody trying to hide their true smell with a bunch of perfume. Her hair is in a long braid and her bangs are just kind of flat on her head. Her glasses are not so good on her face, and she stumbles around a lot, spilling things.

"I get it," I say. "I see what you did there."

EVERY MOTHER RAGES SOMETIMES—this is called "parenting." The girl is bossy, her hand on my mouth to stop me from drinking and spoiling her ending, in that order.

My daughter has trouble making friends, of course, capers or no.

———

DEEP IN THE WOODS, the cowboy is triumphant, the inky shape slain. A skulk of foxes escorts him home, where at long last he is reunited with his daughter. She has been waiting for him, all alone, all this time. He hugs her so tight, makes her alphabet soup. He sets up a tent in the living room. He listens to her stories, really listens. Later he tucks her in, traces a cursive message on her bare back when she can't sleep: *I'm here, I'm here, I'm here.* Outside on the porch, the cowboy has set out big bowls of food and water to feed his friends. The inky shape is elsewhere, a slushy mess on the forest floor. The pissed-off panthers bounce out of their trees, quick to slurp up her blood.

DEEP IN THE WOODS a story is not over, in my humble opinion. The inky shape, that terrible bitch, she comes back from the dead. She researches schools, makes doctors' appointments. She pays parking tickets and does the laundry. She enjoys a drink now and then, okay? But the inky shape is not committing any egregious errors. For example, she is not getting laid. No men are coming in and out, no men at all ever. She buys organic fruits and vegetables. She really does clean sometimes. She keeps her hands to herself, and it is so hard. With a dog, you can overtake them. The trainers will tell you this. It's to establish authority, to maintain control. You can't do this with a child—hold their arms at their sides, sit lightly on their chests. Experts agree!

The cowboy will never come home, but he is not wandering, not lost. He's still in Texas, not even very far away. He commands a crew on a derrick in the Gulf, the big empty hulk of his operation deep underwater. He doesn't need the job—he has the kind of money that begets money—but he enjoys living out there. There are miles of handrail, a thousand light bulbs. Sometimes, to boost team morale, he hosts an open mic. He day-sleeps and plays Ping-Pong, puts checks into the inky shape's account. He's in touch for practical reasons, but he has no interest or intent to return, he's made this clear.

Very soon, he will be dead in a painful, mundane way— a ruptured this, a burst that—and even more funds will arrive. How noble of him to provide such a hefty inheritance! I'm still working out that last part—right now it's more wish than plausible ending.

It's quite possible my daughter will disagree with this version altogether. She might say that I've put words into her mouth. Show me a mother who hasn't.

THE SOFT NO

OUR CHOW CHOW, SHASTA, IS going berserk along her fence, barking and snuffling through the knotholes Chip and I pushed out so she can watch over us. She runs as fast as we do, stops when we stop, presses first one eye and then the other out to see the world. Shasta keeps track because our mother is a couch mother who hardly leaves our house. Mom has gotten afraid of the wrong things—Satanists and wide-open spaces, the white trails that spew out behind airplanes. She stays away from the windows and makes Chip and me walk all over God's creation instead of driving us, afraid that some feeling in her foot will give her the urge to ram a crosswalk person with the car.

Where we live is all cul-de-sacs and long driveways, big boxy houses set close to each other. We have flat, dead yards

covered up with bright green sod. By our school there's a
dinky man-made lake stocked with these depressed imported
ducks. This dumb town is known for two things only: the
Buddy Holly statue by the strip mall and the big, big sky.
I hate that stupid statue—just seeing it sticks the whiniest
songs in your head, makes you think of creepy, old-timey
ghosts: poodle-skirt girls and guys with glop in their hair,
all of them dead from something ridiculous like drag racing.
The sky is all right, streaked pink and orange, but it's more
like a lid than a promise. We're nowhere. If you wanted to
leave you'd be driving forever, not toward anything, just
away.

Days this hot belong to us. See us run both sides of this
street, every lawn our lawn. We are sprinkler kids, shoe-
less and soaked through, blistered and noisy, playing duck-
duck-brick while some window mother—not ours—yells
for us to not get concussed. It is boys versus girls, and Chip
and I are the leaders. Our teams are pink and peeling, kids
willing to do whatever it is we say. The rules: no crying, no
aiming for eyes. Base is that stop sign—safe is both hands
wrapped around it.

Duck-duck-brick is just a big name. We mostly throw
dirt, pebbles, stuff we like to lob at the lower half of people,
where it can't do too much damage. But today our stash is
real bricks, small hunks of them that come from DeeAnn
Pith's busted-up mailbox, which was baseballed all to hell
by midnight high schoolers. Her house gets toilet paper in
the bushes and shaving cream on the lawn, once a whole
two-liter of Coke sprayed at the screen door, so it was no

surprise to any of us, DeeAnn included, to wake up to junk mail and catalogs exploded all over. DeeAnn is from a fat, hateable family. What's worse, her dad is everybody's dentist. If you were feeling mean and had a metal bat and a fast car, it's the Pith house you'd target.

But DeAnn's bricks are perfect—they're the reason I shouted her name from the street and made all the other girls promise not to scratch her or anything, not today. We've wheelbarrowed our supply, hidden it behind a wing wall. There is no time to really look at DeeAnn's wide face or be annoyed by how grateful she seems, running with our pack through the mist, ducking from whatever the boys are throwing.

The boys' fire is endless—who knows where they keep their stash? I've been working on my psychic powers. I'd like to be the one the police call in to find missing kids—to solve the tough crimes, like when somebody finds a box of chopped-off pinkie toes or a blanket dry with blood. So far, I can only read my useless brother's thoughts. I can dip in and scan boring stuff off him all day—what sandwich he wants to eat next or which bathroom at school is the best for number two. Sometimes I can even cut right in and say my piece to him, brain to brain. I do this when I have to, when we're at home and Mom is wearing a fitted sheet tight over her head and shoulders like a shroud, naked underneath. Or when she's got her tackle box of makeup open on the coffee table and she's taking herself from day to evening—with fake eyelashes and everything—for no reason at all.

Sometimes I break into Chip even when I don't have to, when I want to say something in two ways at the exact same time, like when I am digging crescents into his forearms, fighting him for the remote control.

Mine! I roar, right inside his stupid skull.

Don't you be commandeering me, he'll say with his mind, annoyed when I cut through his thoughts like that just because I can.

It is not calm enough or still enough for my magic now, everybody screaming in the street, plus I am sure, without cheating even, that this game is a dead heat, boy and girl lineups perfectly paired, all of us giving it our all. We are glorious, every one. Even DeeAnn Pith is pulling her weight, of which there is a lot. My brother's boys hut-hut and Hail Mary, get good spirals out of their throws. We girls dodge and tumble, take running starts for our cartwheels, our handsprings and punch fronts.

The mom who isn't ours is still going on, yelling from her window about SPFs and ant beds. Her voice is a kind of thrum in your head that makes you meaner. I spin a chunk shot-put style and catch slack-jawed Wesley Ellis in the crotch. My sun-blind brother upholds his best friend's honor, fires an underhander at my heart. Fat chance! I am so, so quick. Baked clay buckshots the sidewalk where we're standing and slivers into our girl feet.

Wesley Ellis wears wind shorts and no underwear, and when he sits, you can see everything about him stuck to his sweaty thigh. He smells like pee, and when he comes to sleepovers at our house, he leaves before bedtime. "I need my beauty rest" is what Wesley Ellis says, his mother looking down at her feet on our front porch.

The heat has all of us riled and screaming, the arching water from the hoses gone warm. A new kid's glasses go flying, then he skids out. "Man down!" Chip says. Our street—it slopes. A misstep and you go rolling. Chip makes a T with his hands and says the word that makes us stop and watch from slick grass. Little clots of new hair sop out under his arms. My ponytailed team looks to me to see if I am still slinging. I make like a heap has already left my hand, brother bound. Chip takes it hard in the shoulder and doesn't flinch. There are times when I don't hate him all that much.

I see that Glasses is hunched up and sweaty, with hands feeling his empty face. His eyes are watering like he's working himself up to break a rule. Wendy Popov, one of my best girls, snakes her foot into a flower bed and comes out with something clenched in her toes. She brushes off her anty leg, tries to make good.

"They're not cracked," she says. "Just weedy." Wendy puts the glasses on Glasses's face, parts his sweaty hair one way, then the other. She gives his back a pat.

Too little too late—Glasses spits a tiny blob of blood into his palm and holds it out for us to see, a little red streak that ruins everything. He wails, and it is a serious sound. The game is over. Where does my brother find these donkeys?

But the game was incredible! The game was amazing! Brain to brain, I shout, *Victory! Victory for the girls!* to my brother. He squints at me, opens his mouth fast to pop his jaw.

Then it's time to put our teams into high-five lines. "Get up," Chip tells Glasses, who is snotty and drippy, squatting on the grass. Glasses looks at my brother but doesn't move. Chip says, "Get. Up." His voice is scary calm, like when a psycho in a movie is about to lose it on somebody. Glasses whimpers and takes his place at the end of the boys' line.

When Chip gives us the signal, we rush our teams past each other and all of us say, "Good game, good game," when we slap hands. You have to look your opponent right in the eye or else the line starts over. You have to mean it. Satisfied, Chip and I tell our teams to go on home. DeeAnn Pith lags behind me, asks what I'm doing next. I swat her away like a big, slow fly.

"I thought I was coming to y'all's house to play," Dee-Ann Pith says. I tell her there have been plenty of times I thought I was going somewhere that I wasn't.

"Get used to it, girl," I say.

Wesley Ellis wants to come over, too, and I hear my brother putting him off.

"My spirit is swinging," is what Mom said when she sent us out this morning. Maybe it is swinging way up high or maybe not, but Chip and me need to get a feel for things before we start bringing people indoors. When the spirit is soaring, our mom is a yes mom or a soft no mom, the kind who lets us get away with anything. We'll have a dozen kids over, sliding down the stairs on a piece of cardboard like a sled. Mom will pace the halls in her clicky heels, flirty on the phone with one of her computer men, her voice a song we follow from room to room. Then she'll sit on the floor with us like a cool big sister or babysitter, chewing gum and playing records, our friends staring shyly at her bouncy hair and perfect jeans. Spirits up, she lets us dig through her purse and order a whole pizza for everyone, even one for Shasta—pineapple and pepperoni, her favorite. Downswing is different: Mom unshowered in dark lipstick and baggy underwear, whimpering in the kitchen, stepping all over the groceries she ordered but won't put away.

If it were my decision, Wesley Ellis would be banned from our house for life, no matter the swing. He thinks he's so smart. He says that in some countries, Shasta would be a meat dog, sliced up in a bowl of rice. When he and Chip play video games, when Mom gets dressed up for nobody and limps around the living room, asking which shoe we like better, Wesley Ellis smirks and says, "Well, Donna, I guess that depends on where you're headed tonight." He teaches my brother awful stuff like cat brains.

"C'mere and see these cat brains," they say to me and the other girls, but we know better than to look by now. "Wanna see some bubble gum?" they try, cupped hands low in front of their crotches. I don't know how boys can walk around being so disgusting, doing nutsack tricks all day.

Shasta is yelping and clawing at the fence because she knows the game is over and she can't see where we're standing. I wish sometimes I could use my magic on her, read her dog thoughts, tell her she's got a treat coming, or ask her why she thinks she can lick the sparkle off the sidewalk.

My scalp aches where earlier Chip forced me to the ground, my ponytail in his fist. My feet are starting to sting, too, all the hurt catching up at once. It's my one chore to turn off the water hoses and reel them in, but I can't be bothered today. Let our grass get soggy. See if I care. Chip says I'm lazy, that it's not fair, then threatens me with the bucket of bagworms he has picked off the juniper bushes. Bagworms is his one chore.

"I got my work done," he says. "I'm accountable." He talks this way, but Chip only does exactly whatever he wants.

To show Chip I am not afraid of him and his gross bucket, I snatch it from him and put it on the grass in front of me, then stomp my bare foot right into it. The bagworms split apart and their juice spews out. I kick my drippy foot up at DeeAnn Pith, who is horrified, still standing with one hand on base. Chip says I am loony tunes, but he is laughing. He is proud of anyone who stands up to everyone.

Chip and I turn away from DeAnn and Wesley and we go up our lawn, dragging and hungry for lunch. Mom might be waiting by the door to blink her phony lashes at us, open her eyes wide, and ask us which one looks weird. But they'll both look weird, in different ways, one with a black line swooping crooked and thick, the other swiped with too much shimmery blue, like the side of a fast fish. Chip will look at Mom's face to see how he should feel. Maybe she'll say she has a new palette she wants to try on me. I hate the way the makeup chokes my skin, but I'll break into Chip and ask, *Do I have to?* and Chip will say back with his brain, *Please, please, I'll owe you.* She'll start smearing me with greasy colors. "We'll do ultramarine all over and scuba in the crease," she'll say. "I can't wear these hues myself. You're a spring. Your daddy was a spring. Chip and me are falls."

If it's all yeses, then I'll invite DeeAnn Pith and Wendy Popov over to say "Peggy Sue" ten times with me in my dark bathroom mirror. If you make your voice gravelly enough and do the devil horns just so, you get to see your own dead face doused with blood. And Chip and Wesley Ellis will play Mexican shrimp hunt, which is just this game where they run around screaming, "*¡Camarón!*" trying to poke up everyone's butts with their shrimpy thumbs.

Or Mom might be locked into her lighted mirror, spreading pastel colors on her tired face, closed to the world, her delivered ice cream melting in the front hall. Or else, worse, she won't be able to make her hands move, and she'll just be sitting on the couch looking stunned, watching TV people kiss and hold each other's faces.

Shasta is gone from her fence now, waiting for us to let her in the back door, or else she's down in our drained swimming pool where there's shade, scraping her blue tongue at the concrete. Inside the front hall, Chip punches for bad guys who might be hiding behind the long burgundy drapes, and I throw open the coat closet to check for psychos. We can't hear Mom, not yet, but the house is cold, AC blasting. It feels so good. Chip and I look at each other and then we go into the living room together, waiting to see what kind of a house we've walked into.

WE DON'T COME NATURAL TO IT

SUKI AND ME, WE'RE HUNGRY and mean. We've got bitter jewels buzzing in our guts. They're bright and gaudy, and we couldn't ignore them if we wanted to. We don't want to. It's the starving that makes us glow—the gimcrack ache, that's what Suki calls this. It's dark and shining, nothing like what you have, what your everyday snack seeker has. It's not a pang. What we've got cuts diamond sharp.

We're carbon slips flitting through customer service. We're silent over raked carpet, sly and tiny with that report you wanted. Would we mind doing this or that? Some days it takes the two of us both to empty a wastebasket, two of us to change the toner in the fax.

We've got thinspiration pinned to our bulletin board. A

lingerie girl eased back in a storm, rain pooling in the bowl of her hip bones. "Ooo la-la," says a pudgy from Accounting, come to hike up the AC. "Hey, pretty-pretty" is what he says to the girl we've spread on cork. He plants a thumb on her face and sucks in sharp. Some clown mustached her, inked her with a monocle and a cigar. We suspect it was one of the cows in Biz Dev, maybe the abdominous mailman.

"See with your eyes, walrus," Suki says to the pudgy. I swat him away with my letter opener, but this pudgy is one of the good ones. He knows to keep his doughnuts out of our department. We've seen how he watches us. He knows we take our coffee black. We'll crank up the heat as soon as he leaves, and this pudgy won't pester us again. Suki and me, we're always so chilly.

I don't mind about the magazine girl's face, but Suki does. I have red nostrils and gums that bleed. I have a white scar above my eyebrow in the shape of an eyebrow. I'm not beautiful in whole like Suki is. Not long ago, I wasn't even beautiful in part, but I'm getting closer. Now, when men stare, I see the bending and folding they do to me from my neck down.

I fought to keep the girl pinned, fucked-up face and all.

We have tricks. High heels double calories spent. Avoid elevators, escalators. Wear a headset when you take the angry calls. Pace during each complaint. Pace during each resolution. Never, ever lick an envelope.

I'm turning sideways in every reflective surface, searching. I'm heading to where Suki has already been, where she is trying to get back to. Inside her desk there is a pair of leather pants pressed and folded in a hanging file labeled "THIS WAS YOU."

RUSSEL IS ALL TALK.

"He ain't gonna do it," Suki says. "He's what they call pseudosuicidal."

Russ drinks St. Ides from a paper bag, sulks around on PATH train platforms. Every six minutes, he loses his nerve fresh. "He's gutless," Suki says. "His body won't let itself leap."

Russ is Suki's man. She has him on speakerphone, to show me what her life is like. We are on lunch, painting our fingernails black in the conference room. I do Suki's right hand and she does mine. "He just needs to talk it out of his system," she tells me.

Listen to him: "I'm getting spinelesser all the time. I'm the worst kind of candy-ass, Suk. I'm getting to be a poltroon."

Suki unmutes us. "Do what now?" she says.

"And the nightmares." Russ says. "Taunts from the universe. I can't put words to them."

"Well," Suki says, "try me." She blows on her fingertips. We have half an hour to kill. There's a yellow peanut M&M on the floor by the umbrella stand.

Russ is a Memphis remnant Suki brought with her. It's hard to believe he's her first and only, that he's had her locked down since high school. I try to hate him, but he's a nice enough guy, pleasant and all that. Once they dragged me bowling with them. I didn't want to be the third wheel, but Suki insisted, said they were sick of each other's company. She and Russ were new to the city like me, and they looked and sounded like home. That's the night I told the beginnings of some lies I'd have to maintain, namely, that I had a boy, too, one I couldn't drag out of the South.

"Is it true," Suki asked with Russ at the top of the bowling lane, posed out of earshot, "that everything's bigger in Texas?" She leaned over the ball return, said, "Tell me, woman to woman." We gabbed and gabbed while Russ bowled for all of us that night.

But then his thoughts got too messy, and he showed Suki his darkest worst. Now, when he isn't failing at being dead, he plays percussion in an urban jug band. He sits on a bucket by the stairs and irks commuters. He's got those clanky spoons and that hollow birdhouse thing you scratch with a stick. At the end of the night, the band divvies up what's been dropped into an open banjo case. Russ goes home and flops into bed with Suki, who shivers up sharp and cold under his bloat.

Russ is still carrying on over the speakerphone, crying a little, spewing about blue devils and haunted haircuts and a baby made of oak. He's like this when he drinks, Suki says. Our nail polish starts to dry. Later we'll go at it with our thumbs, chip it off to make like we don't give a goddamn.

"You're homesick is all" is what Suki says, her eyes rolling, her hands wringing a neck out of the air in front of her.

Then, just like that, Russ says she's probably right. He hangs up and we hang up and Suki gives a little shrug and says, "See what I mean?"

I DON'T MISS TEXAS, but I miss quiet.

It's not cruel to keep a dog penned up, my fatty neighbor says.

"A cage mimics a den," says the fatty, defensive in the laundry room, belligerent in the hall. "A natural place of rest when the pack is still."

But his hound is alone in a kitchen, baying for her brethren while the fatty works the third shift. The bitch can hear me on my side of things. She digs and snuffles at the corner where my wall touches hers. By the sound of her, the moon's full or she's in heat or both. A kick at the wall gets you not a minute of peace.

I swear I won't go out.

Longing wakes me up and keeps me up. Gimcrack ache is a Southern thing, Suki says, but I'd never heard the expression before. It's the feeling you get when you see a bauble on somebody, a cheap necklace or a stickpin so pretty you'd do anything to steal it.

The pain's not gleaming without Suki. It throbs. What I need is her holding out a piece of string as big as her waist was little. I need a picture of her zipped up in those leather pants. It's too late to call her. Russ has probably finished blubbering by now, is fast asleep in a tangle of snot and Suki's hair. I pull my magazines out, my glue stick, get my girls cut and pasted pretty. My kitchen's the safest place. Nothing here but ice.

IT'S SOME COW'S BABY shower. There's a cake and all that. Vanilla or yellow, we couldn't say. We chipped in, but Suki and me don't get close enough to know.

You should hear this cow complaining about the state of the world. Nobody offers her a seat on the bus, nobody opens her doors for her.

"Maybe they can't tell you've got a bun in that oven," Suki says to the cow, and the cow takes it as a compliment and touches Suki's hand, and Suki and me will snort long and hard over that one.

The other cows crowd around the conference table and moo about diaper creams and titty creams, and Suki and me fold our clean sporks into our empty plates and sit on the floor to listen. We jot on pink napkins everything that's too stupid to forget.

Big Boss comes in and gives the cow a card he made everybody sign. Then he flashes his beaver grin and gets ready to shut the party down. He digs at a molar and looks at the gunk under his nail. He burps a little but makes like it's a hiccup, then says, "Back to work, ladies."

"What a parcel of a man," Suki says when he's gone. "What a charmer."

One of the cows gives her a look, since everyone knows Suki is swore to Russ. Before things got bad he bent down on a knee and gave her a gold band. It's all rolled up with Scotch tape on her tiny finger.

"Congratulations" was what I said when she first showed it to me. I worked hard to keep my eyes bright and my voice spirited.

"A ring don't plug a hole," Suki says to the cow, and we snort.

UPSTAIRS, THERE'S A JUNKIE stewardess, thin as a penny. She works the red-eye. I know she's awake by the mess of wire hangers she drops on her closet floor. There's some loony down by the trash cans going through recycling, counting his future quarters aloud. The super's another one. He trolls all hours with a set of keys clinking, flaunting his access. You can pick his comings and goings out over the telenovelas that spill into the halls.

Back home my neighbors were neighbors only in theory. Their houses were too far to walk to, nothing but crouched shapes down long dirt roads marked "Private." I'd drive to the bank of postboxes off the farm route and see their names next to mine, but they were just my best guesses, people I imagined based on what I could see of their mail: fishing catalogs and debt relief offers, poorly designed church promos with words like "RISEN" and "SAVED" in drippy red fonts. Once there was a letter with "U.S. Penitentiary—Max" as the return address. I thought hard about ripping that one open, making it look like a machine took a bite.

Being alone never bothered me back then. I'd step out into my yard at any hour with a cold beer and a feeling like I could walk as far as I'd like and be just fine, nobody to hurt me, nobody I could use to hurt myself. The sky there is filthy with stars, the night so quiet you can hear your blood whooshing around. Even the bobcats—who, no lie, sound exactly like women getting fucked—can't disrupt such perfect nothing. Their satisfied screams draw clean lines around the silence, keeping it safe.

Here there's competing music from everywhere, always. Honking and the train and delivery trucks. Car alarms. Gunfire or fireworks, who can tell?

No point in going out.

In the city you best keep your hackles up. It's not only men to watch for. There are crazy bitches with scissors waiting to cut off your ponytail and sell it to the wig shop. There are sick midgets disguised as kids. Look for patchy hair on their necks, little dicks that stick straight out when they walk.

RUSS PLAYS AT DISAPPEARING. He'll say he's done with this rattrap, ready to pack up and get back to his mama and the opossums in the trees.

"Don't you come after me," he tells Suki, and Suki will say, "Huh?" because she can't hear over the elliptical machine she rides in their living room. She calls it her horse, and she never misses a night with it.

Russ says, "Stay put, Suk." Then he slams off and comes right back because he forgets his keys or wants his dinner.

"Gone whoring" is what Suki says this time, when two days pass, then three. "Somebody skinnier, somebody prettier," she says.

There's nobody like that. I ask does she want me to come stay with her? She says she feels something like carsick, like trying to sleep on your back in a rocking boat. But do I know what? she says. It's not so bad, being alone.

"My offer stands" is what I say.

All this takes place by telephone, me at my kitchen table, Suki at hers.

IT GETS TO WHERE you want to swallow something that isn't even for eating. Like a pot holder can set you off, a grocery bag. You think about cracking up a china plate and sucking on the pieces.

I'm staying in, I swear it.

Where I'm from, falling asleep is easy. You can hear your eyelashes swipe the pillow. There's so much nothing pouring in, you drift off listening to your choice. Foghorns or sportscasters or somebody whispering your name, clear as any bell or bird. Here, I get sleepy doing maps in my mind over the din. It helps to think about which of your morning selves will get you where you're going the fastest. Suki walks to work. She leaves with the sun and comes into the office all shimmery. If she can't catch her breath, she'll lie down under her desk with her feet on a stack of phone books. She'll put her hand in her shirt, grab around for her vitals. Sometimes I'll touch my palm to her forehead, check her for fever. I act like it's some platonic favor to her, like it's just this normal friendly thing I'm doing.

It's when I'm between work and home, coming by train or going by bus, that I'm most afraid.

It's been a week. Russ doesn't come back and doesn't come back. Suki says it's the easiest two hundred pounds she's ever lost.

I'M PACING WITH SOME mister in my ear. He's threatening me with the Better Business Bureau, asking where do I get off selling a touch lamp without the shade? Asking what, exactly, is this scheme?

I'm flipping through the catalog, offering this mister something, anything that compares to what it is he's looking for. Lately, there's a sound when I breathe. A rasp that doesn't quit. The mister's saying, "Put the shade guy on." I patch him into oblivion, the never-ending hold loop Suki and me set up for cranks and perverts.

Russ keeps being gone, and even his mama hasn't heard from him. Where's the police report? Where's the search party? Suki won't mention it, so I won't, either. I keep looking for signals from her, a door that might open differently for me.

There is something eggy in the ashtray by the elevator

bank. The need I've got has corners. It's top-heavy and turning.

SUKI WINDS HER SCARF around her head and waits for me in the lobby.

"Want to come over to my place?" I say. "It's a good little jaunt. Get some steps in."

She's looking at her reflection in the glass of the crappy seahorse painting Big Boss picked out. He's made the whole goddamned lobby ocean themed, shells in glass bowls and little turquoise pillows dumped all over like underwater turds. Suki's using a tiny doe-foot wand to slick hot-pink gloss onto her lips. She smacks her mouth open, smiles, and tilts her chin at herself. "Isn't tonight when you talk to your boy?" she asks. I'm flipping off the lights one by one.

"Looks like that didn't work out so hot," I tell her.

"Oh, honey," she says, and turns to me. Her big eyes are glittery. "So sorry to hear it."

I wind my scarf around like Suki's and shrug.

"Long distance is tough," I tell her. "Started to feel like I didn't really know him."

I look at Suki's mouth and put my pink lip gloss on by feel.

"Still," she says, "I know you had high hopes." Then she yawns.

"A walk?" I say. "Coffee?"

"Let's rain-check it," Suki says. "I've seen my future, and it's a good book and a hot bath."

THOSE NIGHTTIME BOBCATS SOUND scary, but really they're harmless. They won't come near you unless they're starving. Roadkill draws them out, dog food rotting in a metal bowl. It's easy enough to keep them away. Clear your throat and off they go. For the truly stubborn ones, make yourself big—spread your arms out like wings.

Locking eyes with the wrong person is what gets you into trouble here.

There's a look you can give on a train, out on the street. It's the opposite of safe. Safe is eyes down watching your hands. Tucking your hair under your hat, walking fast.

The body hankers for touch, and these people see it all over me. Smell it.

"You miss your stop?" someone will say. I could keep walking, but I won't. The brave ones ask, and I say yes. Yes to the beard in the leather jacket. Yes to the acned teen, the banker in tweed, yes to the off-duty guard guarding nothing now.

"I like your boots," they'll say, and something spreads open. It's the look of want on their faces that decides for me. The body puts itself out for the taking. What comes next can't be stopped, a kind of vomiting.

"You like more than that," I say.

Doorways, alleys, anybody's car.

Yes, yes. All of you, yes.

———

SUSPENDERS IS FULL OF sausage, as per usual. No women except Suki and me and our whore of a waitress. We go there after work with Big Boss and some pudgies because why not?

Suki says, "We're single, am I right?"

Our waitress isn't pretty, isn't fit, but everyone in the bar stares at her like she's something. Suki and me order dry martinis and smoke cigarettes to cancel out the calories. Turns out your body burns heat just trying to breathe.

Suki wears the leather pants. "How do you get into those?" Big Boss says.

Suki says, "It ain't easy," and snorts at me. Then she's drunk and stupid, and the pudgies take turns dipping her on the dance floor.

She takes a breather between numbers. She's down to bones on that barstool, her face pointy against my shoulder. On the bar, the rims of our glasses touch. Nothing has happened between Suki and me. Nothing will.

"I know you're ticked," she whispers. "But just keep working and I swear, you'll meet your goal." The gin feels cold all the way down.

Suki makes a mess flicking olives at our waitress.

RUSS ISN'T DEAD OR dying. He's in the Catskills, clearing his head, pissing off woodpeckers with his drivel. He's back in touch, and aren't we all just so relieved?

"We're giving it another go," Suki says to me, and shrugs.

At lunch, she gets him on speed dial, says, "Here's the horse's mouth."

Russ says he's lost and found. Was blind but now he sees. He's got a bandaged wrist and a fresh outlook.

"Howdy, Russel," I say into the speakerphone. "I'm glad you're such a chickenshit."

RUSS TAKES US OUT for barbecue, his treat. The place is fancy, with a line of tourists down the block. I wonder how much busking he had to do to afford this, how many intolerable kazoo covers it took.

I can't bring myself to seem appreciative, even when Russ holds the door open for both of us, even when he keeps asking me, "You good?" about my headache and the wait time for a table and me not talking much. I wonder if he'll pay the check with crushed dollar bills and germy coins. I'd feel guilty, but his generosity is mostly show—Suki and me are cheap dinner dates.

The restaurant is known for spit pigs and a legendary dry rub, but Russ has chosen this place to pick it apart. "No way they have the soul in this city to do it right," he says. We get a booth at the back, and I sit across from them. I'm in full third-wheel glory, trying to think of something to say. Russ has got a new beard and a suntan, his scabby wrist resting on the table until I stare at it too long.

He scoffs at the boot-wearing waitstaff, the gourmet

mustard on the tables. There's fancy taxidermy all over, a lasso and spurs in a pine shadow box. "No potato salad," he says, poring over the menu. "Fennel chimichurri. Good God."

Suki and me keep our menus facedown, then hand them over quick. We ask for Diet Cokes, no lemon, that's it. Russ interrogates the waitress and eventually rattles off his order. He gives each dish its full name, thick with hate: bore riblets with honey and sambal, three-cheese truffle macaroni, kaleslaw, brisket with plums and port.

"Oak-smoked or grilled?" the waitress asks, and Russ looks up at her bewildered, like he might cry, the joke gone too far.

He finally says, "Surprise me," and the waitress smirks and trots off. Suki doesn't know it, but her foot is mashing mine under the table, her hot leg pressing against my shin from time to time.

We'll go bowling after this, then out for beers. I tell myself I'll leave early, but if they'll have me, I'll follow them home. I won't leave until Suki starts yawning, once Russ is asleep in front of the TV and she has brushed and flossed her teeth, changed into the big T-shirt she wears for bed.

"Tell me y'all have normal pickles," Russ calls out to nobody.

Suki laughs and picks up his hand, kisses the tough knuckles. He pulls her close to him on the bench seat. "You're just a little shrimp," he says to her. "When'd you get so shrimpy?" She's chewing sugarless gum, same as me, and she giggles and pops a bubble in his face. I shred a napkin for a while, ogle a busboy. I try to point my desire at him, make it look like I am looking hard at the small muscles in his arms, the graceful way he holds the high tray of gory plates. Russ touches Suki's face, sticks his nose in her ear. I can smell ribs already, foresee them falling off hot bones.

It's torture, all of it. Some other, smarter me is a thousand miles away, back home on the edge of hardpan pasture, eating a ham sandwich. Or at least in another part of this city, nourished and well rested, making healthy choices in a grocery store, happy alone, not hanging on to anybody.

"You good?" Russ says to me.

My minty gum liquefies under my tongue. The bread basket appears, a terrible miracle in the center of the table, its heaping sidecar of hand-churned butter.

"Get. Away," Suki says, and pushes it over to Russ.

He maims a roll, scrapes on a heavy pat of butter. He grimaces at the first bite. "Sourdough," he says. "Jesus Christ."

I wait for Suki to give me the look that says we are separate from the rest of the world. Russ chews and swallows and chews.

There's a jukebox playing young country. " 'Course there is," Russ says, aggravated, finishing his fistful of wrong bread. He rifles in his pocket and dumps diseased change on the table in front of me.

"Oooh," Suki says to me. "Do it."

He wants to be alone with her. They both want it, why pretend otherwise?

I pump quarters into the machine. The jukebox is garbage with one exception, a duet I punch in six times in a row. It starts to play, so familiar and special to me it's like somebody has plugged a speaker right into my stupid heart.

"I love this one," Suki says when I get back to the table.

"I know it," I say. Russ's food has arrived, artful and steaming on a big oval plate. I slide into the booth choked with woodsmoke and paprika, chipotle, brown sugar. "Looks all right," I say, ashamed by how wet the words sound, how ready my mouth is.

Then I see that Suki's hands have been all over Russ's plate. There's expensive macaroni on her sleeve.

"Want some?" she asks me, sheepish.

"Nah," I say. "No. Nope." My song is too far away, the woman's voice coming in and out like a swinging skirt, the man's part mostly gone, his lowest notes dropped flat on a dirty floor.

Suki and Russ work around the plate. Russ's jaw pops. Suki smacks.

"It's bullshit, but it's so good!" she says to me.

Russ sucks his teeth and says, "Too sweet."

Suki shovels in kaleslaw. She drips riblet grease on the checkered tablecloth, licks burgundy sauce off her ring finger. Russ feeds her huge forkfuls of the complicated brisket. It's quiet at the table except for her smacks and hollers, little yelps of astonished satisfaction.

"Bourbon?" I say. "Right?"

Suki swallows. "Smart," she says.

"Right?" I look for the smug waiter.

"Fine with me," Russ says, his lips sticky, a sheen of fat on his chin. He tips his near-empty plate to show me a sprig of sage caught in bright orange emulsion.

"Ridiculous," he says.

MY KEY IS GONE, or I never had it. It's late, early. I buzz the super. Nothing. Where I'm from there's no point in locking your door.

I buzz the fatty, and I buzz the junkie stewardess. They're sleeping sound or have already gone to work. I've got something like wet gauze in my gut, soaked up and bloating.

Next I start in on people I don't know, apartment numbers that seem friendly somehow. I'm pleading to the groggy and the curious. The trick is to take your demands and make them sparkle.

"We've got a floor plan in common" is what I'm saying, trying to say. The gauze grows, a toilet the only answer. They're ignoring me, my neighbors. I'm buzzing everybody now, moving down the list. I don't discriminate. Morse code, dots and dashes, then I'm mashing with my fists, my forearms, really giving it my all. Now they're saying they'll get the cops involved or else come down and show how mad they are. Some of them are oddly specific about solving this buzzer deal, each one with a different method or threat.

A bathroom. Jesus. I start moaning into the intercom, to

prove how serious and how crazy. It frees me up, the sound of big need coming from my face like that. I have no idea why, but the noise seems to get a better response from folks. I can hear some of them breathing, waiting. I'm haunting my way through the building. "It's me" is what I say when I stop my yowl to listen. "It's me, it's me, it's me."

THE LIGHT
WILL POUR IN

SHE HAD HER HEART SET on a coast—didn't matter to her which one—but we'd started to limp in the slow middle of nowhere. We were down to sock money, and nothing was easy, now that we'd left real life behind. We had turned our losses inward, at each other, and now we fought, mostly on buses or at bus stations or on looping walks through hateful, sprawling towns, looking for the terminal.

These weren't knock-down-drag-outs like we had when we were alone, behind the closed doors of whatever shitbox motel or rented room. Just offhand fuck-yous over everyday things, with most of the bad feelings triggered by hunger or lack of sleep. Trish liked to pick at me with questions. She posed them in a kind of singsong innocence meant to cut.

Like how had I lived such a long, long life without know-ing the One True Way to pack a suitcase? And how much torrential rain had to fall before I'd hold up a newspaper or my jacket or something, anything, as a kind of gentlemanly shield over her?

It was my fault, Trish insisted, that we were stuck in this southern swirl. There is no excuse, when you're traveling by bus, for not knowing where the bus station is. But we'd show up somewhere in the dark and go one way for a burger and another for a place to sleep, and by morning we'd be aimless, the whole world completely remade in the sunlight.

We started sitting rows apart on whichever night bus was cheapest, whisper-fighting past the sleeping heads of strang-ers. Once we had hurt each other enough we'd slump down, sit forlorn with our thoughts in the lurching dark. Then we'd get lonesome. Because she knew it was my weakness, Trish would start humming, soft and dreamy, a child trying to put herself to sleep. These were drowsy little tunes that went nowhere, songs mixed up with squeaking bus. What came out of her was sweet and clear, nothing like the voice she used for complaining about every damn thing. I'd miss the shape of her mouth, how her lips are always slicked with something shimmery, how her tongue taps at her chipped front tooth. I'd know her hands were in her tangled hair, moving. I hated the thumpy road and the noisy brakes, the awful bodies shifting and coughing, all the unbearable peo-ple who weren't her.

I'd wobble up or down the aisle and glower at the man

slid in tight beside her—and it was always a man, believe me—until the idiot, slack-jawed and staring, turned from her and saw something serious in my face. Finally he'd sigh and gather up his mess—his Bigfoot tabloids, his feed bag of corn chips—and go sit somewhere else. Trish would give me the finger but then finish singing just for me. We'd say our sorrys and cozy up—play cards or grab ass or just sit there and watch a lot of moonlit nothing stream by.

One night we passed a giant billboard for a tequila brand—a moist drink in a woman's grip, her tan legs spread out before a frothy sea. Trish is one of those girls with blue fingertips, always shivering. She leaned into me, hugged herself with her little chicken arms, and pointed at the fake sun. "I'm gonna buy a big, floppy hat, first thing," she said. "Park my butt in some sand and just sit and sit."

There is a not-small part of me that can't help but see a thing through to its disappointing end.

TO KEEP THINGS SMOOTH with Trish—because what choice did I have, lovestruck, out on the edge of some strange metroplex?—I checked us into one of those hotels where the rooms have kitchenettes. It was the nicest place so far, a well-known chain with an ice machine, no bulletproof anything, anywhere. I figured we'd take a break, live like kings until the money ran out, then worry about what else.

Trish asked the front desk clerk if there was a pool. When he said there wasn't, she sighed with her whole body and tromped off to go pout by the travel brochures.

"Got three teenagers myself," the clerk said, and lifted his eyebrows at me. "All girls."

Trish snorted behind me, doubled over at the thought. Some people just can't keep their goddamn assumptions in. My ears rang while the clerk pecked on the computer with one finger, said he was working out a double room for us on the ground floor. I made a quick choice between getting into details or getting into bed. I filed the guy under Dumb Fuck, imagined what it might feel like to grab him by the throat. Then I thought about my chins and my soft gut, all the gray in my hair. I had a notch in my stomach where the top of my belt buckle pressed into me, a little pink gash of half-moon that chafed and itched and got deeper or shallower but never went away. And next to me, drawing the cruelest of comparisons, was Trish: not a teenager, Dumb Fuck, but young and gorgeous, dewy and lithe, chomping her gum and rolling her eyes, snapping the room key out of my hand.

"Come on, Daddy," she said to me, her hip cocked.

The whole place smelled like bleach. "Speak-a-dee English?" I said to a brown housekeeper in the hallway.

"Take whatever," she said, not a trace of accent. She shook her head at me but gestured all over the cart she was pushing. I helped myself to her fresh towels, her teeny toothpastes and lotions. Embarrassed, Trish pretended not to know me, glided past while I stockpiled.

"You got those little liquor bottles in the rooms?" I asked the girl, soft so Trish couldn't hear. "Y'all sell that stuff here?"

"No, sir," she said. "We don't."

"That's fine," I said. "That's a good thing."

Trish turned the key in the door, and I pushed through with our bags and my haul. "It's perfect," I said. "One bed for sleeping and one bed for you know what." It would be a treat to turn back the covers and not see pubes from every stripe of person.

Never happy, Trish glared at the art above the beds, a dead-eyed watercolor deer split into two frames.

"You think that's in all the rooms?" she said. "Or are we just lucky?" She unwound her pale hair, raked her fingers through the incredible length.

"I'll take the ass end," I said, and threw my jacket on the far bed. "You know me." I did that thing where you grin bigger than the joke deserves.

I sat down and turned on the TV while she skulked around the room. On the back of the remote was a list of all the channels. I read them off, one by one. TV was something I missed. Heads delivering bad news, stupid laugh tracks on top of stupid situations.

"Wanna watch something, T?"

She squinted at a faint cigarette burn in the wallpaper, touched it like an elevator button. "Cartoons or animals," she said. "I'm sick of people."

Her eyes were resting everywhere, judging everything, no shame. She opened the mini fridge, pulled out a box of Arm & Hammer with the corner ripped off. She stuck her nose in deep for a whiff.

"Christ almighty," she said, and jerked back.

She made a big show of dumping the baking soda into a trash can by the door, poured it high like a loose bartender so that a white cloud puffed up and floated around. She faked a coughing fit, closed the fridge, opened the closet.

"You want me to order up some food?" I said.

I kept my voice steady. I was doing my counting trick. I was doing the breathing thing. I conjured an alternate Trish from our early days, a Trish impossible to hate. A Trish in a daisy printed dress, smiling sweetly over her shoulder.

"There's room service?" she said. She pulled a couple of wire hangers out of the closet and mangled them for no reason, threw them on the floor.

"There's a place down the street," I said. "I'll have them make us a doggie bag."

She sucked air between her teeth. "That fish place?"

"Sign said hush puppies, too," I said. "Shrimp cocktail, I imagine."

"Dallas fish," she said. "Lord, no."

I turned off the TV and went to see about the view. I didn't say that fish is fish, goddamn it—it's all frozen and flown in from someplace else. It was too late to eat anyway.

The window pointed at the parking lot, and there was a guy out there doing some kind of tweaker art project with stuff from the garbage. Most of what he pulled out he'd drop and crunch underfoot, but some of the trash, the junk that spoke to him, I guess, he'd hold up to the streetlight, look at the behind-side of it. Then, with great care, he'd add it to the little heap he was sculpting. Every so often he'd step back to admire his work, then turn away from the wind and cup a flame. I pulled the blackouts shut and the flowery drapes, too. I didn't need to give Trish another thing to rail about.

She frowned and fingered her autograph into the dust on top of the dresser, arced a rainbow with her long white hand. She flipped and flipped the switch on a lamp that wouldn't light. A tag itched me somewhere inside my shirt.

"You done yet?" I said.

She wasn't. She didn't like my tone and she turned and whipped her hair at me, stepped over a tiny stain in the carpet like it was a dead thing. I tried to imagine a Trish so lovely I could touch her with nothing but tenderness. She charged into the bathroom, ready to assess the commode, no doubt, and I stayed close behind her, my jaw tingling. But she let out a yelp of delight when she saw the shower, white tiled and sparkly, a glass door instead of a curtain. She stepped in, shoes and all, belted out a bunch of high, bright notes.

"They've got those itty-bitty soaps, too," I said.

She was warming up, moving through her scales. Back home, she'd been bullied out of church choir because of me, because of us. She must have missed singing in a room that lifted sound like that, sent her voice out and back to her in a swell.

I sat on the toilet to pull off my boots. I rested, breathing heavy from the effort, such a fat fuck. My toenails needed clipping.

Now she was doing, what? *Grease*? *Cats*? She'd played all the best roles in the community theater, but I don't pretend to follow that world. She sang every part, right there in the shower stall, characters not so much singing as talking fast, cutting each other off in tone, explaining their motives. I can do without musicals, but Trish doesn't take requests.

What I loved hearing was the religious music, stuff in Latin, maybe, or stuff in English, but with the words broke apart in weird places. Sundays, I'd sit my wife and kid down in the pew right behind Trish so I could watch the quick blood beat in her neck. In psalms the vowels are whole worlds, so long and slack you forget they're part of something bigger. When she lets it, Trish's voice puts a fullness in you that is beautiful and awful, makes you feel like a glass of something waiting to be spilled.

But this was just *Fiddler on the Roof,* that was it, the one where the three sisters ask the matchmaker to send them their match, make him rich and all that. Only now the sisters were Trish and Trish and Trish and she pantomimed doing chores in the little glass stall—fake scrubbing, sweeping, hanging clothes on a line. She was pretty convincing, considering she had very little experience with housework. Oh, she wanted things clean, but she wasn't going to be the one to do it.

She stripped, kicked her shoes and clothes out of the stall, and turned on the tap. There were tremendous cobalt bruises on her arms, both of them, high in the stringy meat of her shoulders. Those marks should have made me ashamed, but instead I felt a little jolt, like discovering your name tattooed on a lover. Fighting and forgiving was our glue. I felt the same intimacy when I saw the curved white scars all over my forearms, places where Trish had clawed and scratched and dug at me.

She wound her wet hair up like a big blond seashell and made herself slippery. She kept singing that annoying song, doing a kind of exaggerated showering, lots of lathering, big circles for show. Then she bent at the waist, folded herself in half, and watched me from between her soapy legs. It was an invitation.

"Make sure you get them feet," I said.

I thought about my knees, how I wasn't sure if I could stand just yet. I wanted to keep watching her from this angle, and also I couldn't decide how best to work myself up off the pot.

And then, praise Jesus, she was doing a psalm or some kind of gospel. *Holy, holy,* she sang, but it was the way she looked between the notes—mouth open, no sound coming out—that really choked me up.

My signals were crossed, if I'm being honest. All the while she kept doing her little tease, bending as far as a person should bend. The whole deal was not as sexy as she maybe hoped. It made me think of slipped disks, watching her, and my stomach was churning, like my ass knew I was sitting on a toilet. The fluorescents lit her face up kind of scary.

Later, after we settled forever in the sagging center of the state—after Trish had stopped with the beach talk and given up all designs of a life next to big water—this little routine would stand out as the beginning of the dark times. Before she started coming to bars with me for what she called "the spirit of the place," where she'd sit and drink water and eat garnishes and I'd be afraid to leave her alone to take a piss. With every whiskey I'd finish, she'd ask to smell my glass.

The dark times came in that hotel bathroom, and my body knew it before I did. I couldn't get it up. "It's okay," Trish said. "Happens to lots of old guys," and it had happened to me before, had started happening quite a bit. But it wasn't just the way she looked that night, terrifying and angelic and lit from within. We were ruined, permanently, and this was one of many signs to come, a message meant for me especially, glowing neon gas that said: *LET HER GO*. There would be others—dozens, hundreds. At our tiny rented house in Matador, a freaky little cyclone would take our brand-new wind chimes, lift them up and off the porch while we watched. From where Trish and I sat drinking—she was back to drinking by then—we would hear the music of them tinkling around up there, spinning in the dark sky.

INTO THE FOLD

NEW GIRLS, THEY ARE SO braggy, always begging you to look. They unzip their luggage in slo-mo, reach their hands in to pull apart cashmere and silk, stroke the designer prints and patterns all of us recognize. They bring kidskin belts and slouchy boots, lavish jeans stacked flat—everything the latest thing. It is so pointless, all of it a waste. We wear uniforms, and there are no boys here to impress.

Eloise Sheen is the worst one yet, here for weeks and flaunting still. She has something gold to show.

"No touchy," she tells us. "Feast with your eyeballs."

She bends over unbuttoned, says for us to see what her father sent her. She does not say for us to see her sucks, but her sucks are there in her shirt, low and swinging, stealing the show. A necklace is her point.

"From overseas," she says, and don't we know it.

Eloise Sheen is half French and she never lets you forget. She fingernails free every foreign stamp. She re-licks, leaves plants and flags and prime ministers smeary, spit-stuck to the mirror all of us share. These new girls, their guilty parents still send gifts.

"All the rage," she says, and shows us.

It is a fish the size of a real live goldfish. Orange gems are its scales, and a gold chain slides around where eyes should be. Someone says, "Ick," and then all of us looking down Eloise Sheen's shirt say, "Ick," or make faces like "Ick."

Eloise Sheen's upper lip is sweaty when she says, "In France, fish are the richest things going." That is just the kind of thing these new girls always say.

Tanner says, "That's not gold." She says she can spot a fake by the way it spins. Tanner knows. She's getting all kinds of jewelry once some key people in her family die— strands of Akoya pearls longer than her arms, an irradiated green diamond big as a fist. "That's plated, hon," she says, squinting, looking embarrassed on behalf of the whole world.

Then Pepper says, "Stinking plate of fish," and holds her nose, and everybody laughs.

Eloise Sheen is trembly, rubber chinned. It looks like she is getting her guts together to go tattle, so all of us put our arms around her quick and say, "Group hug!" to keep whatever is about to happen from happening.

ELOISE SHEEN HAS THE homesick shits. There is the powder room and there is the can. You can guess which one is for making snake pits, but Eloise Sheen thinks she is an exception. The powder room is the only place in this place with a real lock that locks, not those hook-and-eye shows anybody can bust through or flip up with a pencil.

It is after the first bell and all of us are still sitting on our bunks, waiting to get at the mirror.

"Shake a leg, Stinkbomb," Skylar says to the powder room door. "Push it out."

"Turn on the radio," Eloise Sheen bosses from inside. "Sing something," she says.

"My toothbrush is in there," McKenna whines.

We don't want to do what Eloise Sheen asks, but we also do not want to hear her mess, so we sing the song about Osprey House, our house, the best house here. It is the song where Osprey defeats Eagle and Kestral, only we change Kestral's name to Worst-ral in the song. We sing through our ponytails so we can smell our shampoo instead of smelling Eloise Sheen. We have not come up with an insult for Eagle House yet.

The second bell rings, and we can forget about getting ready for our day. We stop at the door to put on our sneakers: identical white mountain-cut midtops with high tongues and speed hooks. They're from Tokyo, a quilted-leather style that bends school rules as far as they'll go. Tanner's the one who suggested this brand, but the vote was unanimous. Eloise Sheen has, what, Keds or something? French Keds? Our socks are regulation white, nothing fancy.

All of us in Room B have the same schedule. Our day is assembly, class, lunch, class, study hall, bonus. Bonus is horses or swimming, but Eloise Sheen has a note. At the stables, she sits on a post and reads the paper, twists her stupid fish.

Skylar picks Misty, a horse she says her mother used to ride when she was an Osprey. Tanner says for Skylar to have at it. She says in horse years Misty is the living dead. Tanner gets Pippen, the filly we all fight over. I ride asthmatic Raven. Raven is a mare, not a gelding like everybody says. Truth told, Raven is my favorite—what she lacks in speed she makes up for in character.

Lazy Miss Moss leaves the paddock for a cigarette. She says she has something stuck in her eye. We are supposed to keep working on lead changes, but instead we get worked up about the townie who was STABBED TO DEATH at the mall. Eloise Sheen, now perky, waves us over with the headline.

"When Father hears about this," Eloise Sheen says, "it's bon voyage for me."

The girl in the picture is black and white and smiling, our age exactly. The person who did the stabbing was the last person you would think, just an old man in the food court, gone crazy in an instant.

"And that, ladies, is why I only shop in boutiques," Skylar says. Pepper laughs, so all of us laugh.

Eloise Sheen flips to the jump.

"Lung, lung, heart," she says, scanning. "Swiss Army knife."

"Congratulations—you can read," McKenna says, trotting off on Riley, who nobody wants. Riley has a rash under his saddle. McKenna is a baby, a bottom-bunker. Tonight Pepper will make crazy old man sounds and poke her in the dark.

Miss Moss is back, telling Eloise Sheen she is in contempt of the headmistress.

"Don't you think we should know if a killer is on the loose?" Eloise Sheen says.

"Too sick to ride, too sick to read," Miss Moss says. Miss Moss confiscates the newspaper. "They caught him," she says to us. "No cause for alarm—your parents agree."

It is everywhere outside of here that is not safe. When Miss Moss turns her back, Eloise Sheen blows her a kiss and shimmies her massive sucks.

"Less laughing," Miss Moss says to us. "More cantering."

THE GIRLS IN OSPREY Room B want a sexy story. It is moonlit, lights out.

"Not you, Pepper," Skylar says. We have heard the story about Pepper and the lawn boy, Paulie Zinc, one too many times. It is PG-13 at best, and Pepper is a liar.

"What about you, Bazongas?" Tanner says to Eloise Sheen. "Ever put those bazongas to good use?"

Tanner is bent backward at the knees, hanging over Eloise Sheen like a blond bat, blood rushing to her scalp. New girls get the bad bunks, the bottom ones, where someone is always using your bed as a place to sit or else stepping all over you.

Eloise Sheen says Frenchmen are crazy for redheads. She says on the streets they stop to stare, ask her to pose for pictures.

"In Paris," she says, "it's a full-time job for my father to keep them off me."

"Sure," Pepper says. "Right."

"This one guy came up to us in the park," Eloise Sheen says. "He asked me to marry him, said it was love at first sight. All of this in French, of course—*très* sexy. But he got handsy then and there. My father went berserk."

Eloise Sheen boasts that her father has ways of killing a man with one hand. "He's secret service," she says. "That's all I need to say. He knows the head yank and Russian omelet and the hook-to-jaw—"

"Sex," Tanner says. "Where's the sex?"

Eloise Sheen stops talking so loud.

"The sexy guy was handsy," she says.

Eloise Sheen chinks her fake fish along its fake chain. She is not so braggy now.

Tanner sighs and swings herself back up. "Somebody else go," she says.

Nobody says anything, and then McKenna says, "I'm sleepy. Let's sleep." McKenna doesn't have a story. Neither do I.

Then Skylar sits up and does her best Pepper impression: "It's the story of a boy and a girl. It's the story of a lawn."

Later, when all of us are supposed to be sleeping, I hear Eloise Sheen next to me, quaking in her bunk. She is close enough that I could touch her if I wanted. It is true I am also in a bad bunk, a bottom bunk, but part of being an Osprey is patience—everyone says so.

BONUS IS SWIMMING. MISS Drown lets us call her Miss Drown. She wears a polka-dotted one-piece with a little skirt built in. Tanner says this is because Miss Drown does not want anybody seeing her business district. Ospreys wear yellow suits. When we get wet, you can see everybody's sucks, even if they are very small.

All of us, including Headmistress and the teachers, have had it up to here with Eloise Sheen's routine. When she is not shitting, she is sulking or else crying in the bathtub, fully clothed. She is casting Room B in a very bad light. Miss Drown says note or not, Eloise Sheen has to take the swim test, safety first. Miss Drown snaps on her swim cap, regulation black with the gold school crest, and that's that—end of discussion.

"The fish stays on," says Eloise Sheen.

Tanner says, "Don't come crying to us when your neck goes green."

We line up on the dock. The pool is really a roped-off part of the lake. Like everything else on campus, our lake is artificial, probably dug up by an expensive machine, calibrated to be precisely lake deep, perfectly lake-y. The first question of the test is jumping in and letting the water go over our heads. It gets colder and blacker the deeper we go.

The next question is to swim the perimeter while Miss Drown bobs in the middle, barking out the strokes. We do the side, the breast, the trudgen, and the crawl.

"Nice work, ladies!" Miss Drown says.

Everybody passes, flying colors, even Eloise Sheen.

"You've turned out to be quite the swimmer," Miss Drown says to her.

"Fat floats" is what Pepper says, loud enough for all of us to hear.

It is tough to tell tears apart from lake water, and Eloise Sheen sinks under fast.

Miss Drown says, "Ladies!" and Pepper stops smiling, so we stop smiling, too.

All of us are waiting to see where Eloise Sheen will pop up, but when she does she is gone from the roped-off pool, out in the open where Miss Drown says there are underwater trees waiting to tangle and clutch.

Miss Drown paddles off after Eloise Sheen, but Eloise Sheen has her beat. It is a chase in slow motion, Miss Drown and Eloise Sheen just heads on the water, Miss Drown shouting, "Please, let's please turn back."

When Eloise Sheen is safe on the shore in a fluffy white robe, Miss Drown walks down the dock to give us a lecture. We are pruney, still paddling.

"A written apology," she tells us, "stat." All of us are looking out over the water or up at the sky so we do not have to look back at shivering Eloise Sheen or at Miss Drown's disappointed face.

Miss Drown says we are making Eloise Sheen worse.

"I've seen it before," she tells us. "Not pretty."

She says if we do not let Eloise Sheen into the fold, she will become one of those people who spend their days in bed, afraid of showers and jobs, things most people are not afraid of.

WE HAVE PARENTS WHO are bankers and painters and district attorneys—McKenna's mom plays a detective on TV. They are oil parents, cattle and real estate parents. In their time off they are parents who ski and stand on sandbars feeding stingrays, parents who bring clean water to potbellied, fly-speckled orphans. They make education a priority, that is something they will tell you over and over. They send us short letters, postcards mostly. Since the fish, Eloise Sheen's mail has started to look like ours.

Eloise Sheen does not know the trick, and I am not going to be the one to tell her. The trick is to go for a run when you feel that lumpy-throat feeling. Call it exercise, and nobody will notice. If you can pump your legs past Eagle and Kestral, run past the commons and the lake and the paddocks and up into the woods, up to the rocks where the snakes and the snake eggs are, down into the blackberry field where Pepper got her sucks sucked on by the lawn boy, Paulie Zinc—if you can make it past all that without

crying, then you have made it. And if you can't make it
that far, then so what? There is nobody around to see you
shattered.

RAVEN BREAKS FREE AND winds up dead, tangled in barbed
wire. The loudspeaker news comes through in study hall—
someone has been careless, a stall door left open. Tanner
says, "At least it wasn't Pippen," and all the girls agree that
Raven is the second-best death choice after Misty, who will
be dead soon enough. Pepper makes a joke about horse
tartare for dinner, says Hairnet Nancy will pass it off as a
delicacy.

I let the news work its way through me. At first I think
there must be a kind of coincidence, how odd that there
could be two Ravens at one school, one who is brushed and
blanketed in her stall and this new, dead horse I've never
even seen. Then it is like all terrible news—expected, a great
fear confirmed. The light in the room lurches. I am shaking
my head, shaking out the cold loudspeaker voice, the heart-
less Ospreys joking all around. I am on my back on the floor,
looking at the rainbow underside of the table where everybody puts their bubble gum. It is easy enough to tell that an
Eagle is to blame—they had horses last—but the headmistress has not included that fact in her announcement. An
Eagle, of course, those sharks with wings. Real eagles carry
off baby goats, target the weak and weary. Ospreys are no
joke—we'll pull a squirrel apart if we're starving, but never

for sport. We mostly eat fish. Eagles pick up turtles and dash them on the rocks for fun.

I am railing, raving about vengeance and turtle guts. "They'll do it just to hear the crack!" I say all this, somehow, out loud. Something black bobs in my throat.

"Get up," Pepper says, sharp. "What are you, having a seizure?"

And I think maybe I am, but how would I know? This is something like a sneeze, a thing you can't stop from coming. What I know is that everybody is embarrassed, shushing me and pulling me up off the floor.

Then I am running fast, out of study hall and into the commons. I think about pumping my legs past the fake lake and the sad paddocks, over the snaky outskirts, through the sexy berry patch. I'll never make it. Nobody is chasing after me anyway. I want comfort or something close to it. It surprises me, but I run to Osprey House, to Room B.

I don't want to see anybody, least of all Eloise Sheen, but guess who is there, sitting on her bunk when I open the door. She must have left sometime post-horsemeat, pre-turtle spew. It smells like she has been in here all day, missing home. It will serve her well—running so fast.

I climb up top, flop onto Tanner's bunk.

"Watch yourself," Eloise Sheen says, because I have shaken her and stepped on her hand on my way up.

Maybe it is because of Eloise Sheen, but up on Tanner's bed, I cannot get myself to cry. Raven in barbed wire— impossible.

"Everybody really hates you a bunch," I say to Eloise Sheen.

There is a sound that I think is Eloise Sheen rattling her stupid fish, but then I realize it is the sound of paper. Eloise Sheen is holding up a note, waving it between the bars of my bunk—Tanner's bunk, which I am borrowing. I think it is a dumb French letter from her dumb French father.

"Not interested," I say, but she keeps waving the paper, and I see that there is a part she has circled.

"We are sorry," the circled part says. "We like you. Kittredge King is the weirdo." Kittredge King is me. The note is signed by everybody. Eloise Sheen, full of pride, lets me hold the letter.

BLACK LIGHT

JESUS, THAT'S WHO. SHE FOUND Him on the basketball court. No matter she's only a point guard, a B-teamer. She's calling divine intervention from the free-throw line. That's what I'm up against.

"Model or athlete?" asked everybody, always. She'd bend down to listen, then go pink and say, "Neither." Sure, she's tall. People convinced her she was wasting those legs. She wasn't. *You should see her on her back* was what I wanted to tell them. She's endless. A gaggle of girls in jerseys kept her cornered. When they looked at her they saw three-pointers, hands that could palm a ball, no sweat. They got between us between classes, wore her down with their questions. Did she play? Had she tried? She was flattered. She didn't have many female friends other than me. Why would she? I mean, have you seen her?

The Bible bit threw me off. The lot of them swarming the flagpole in the mornings, bringing up the sun with their psalms. I have no idea why sports and religion intermingle—they just do. It seems some people take Jesus for a jock. Soon she was there, too, pressed up against the other thumpers. She was primed, ready to be in His grip. "Let's get right with God," she told me, giddy. "Let's repent!" My girl, going. Gone.

I WAS IN THE throng, in the bleachers on the night in question. I'd just gotten my driver's license and the lonely freedom to drag myself where I knew I wasn't wanted. She took a shot and made it. No miracle there. She'd been practicing, let me tell you. Every phone call thick with her breath, punched out by some kind of background dribble. Every note I passed her was skimmed, then crushed, tossed pointwise at a trash can. When I caught up to her in the hall—no easy feat with those legs of hers—she'd jog in place while we talked, two fingers jammed into the pulse under her jaw, eyes locked on her watch's second hand.

I wore green, clapped when other green people clapped. There was no searing white light. No celestial choir. True, my glasses kept steaming up. True, a bigheaded football type blocked much of my view, but I got the gist. From

where I sat it looked like a bunch of dykes being dykey.
Lady Rams ramming. Hallelujah.

"TAKE IT OUT" WAS what she said when I first got my hand in
her. "Take it out so you can put it right back in." She was a
flood, sopping. A girl like that can't last. A fleeting gleam.
I don't know if there's a word for the ache of missing something when you still have it. I'd kiss her and taste my doom.

I was new in town and thought I was passing. I trudged
alongside her in the same brand of jeans she wore, the same
sneakers. We shared a cylinder of glittery lip gloss, took
turns checking each other's mouths for errant sparkle. Best
friends. We linked arms in the halls. She was safe, but something always gives me away. My voice, maybe. My walk.
Kids laughed as we passed, so apparent was my heart.

AT MY OLD SCHOOL I got punched in the nose for touching
the prom queen's hair. She wasn't my type, if you need to
know. A little too bleached in the teeth, lots of neon in
her wardrobe. Bored in Latin, where else was I supposed
to look? Nothing to do but dream at her from across our
shared desk, study that slow, conjugating mouth. One day
I took it too far, reached to sweep Queenie's bangs off her
brow. Her fist went out quick—a reflex. And I deserved
it, I did. For not knowing the difference between what I
wanted and what I could get in this life, or for knowing and
going for it anyway. More than that, I deserved that punch

for being a weirdo in high school, for breaking the rules. Everyone knows you keep your mouth shut, dress how they dress, like what they like. Don't draw attention to yourself. Don't fucking *touch* anybody, moron, especially not a girl like that. Too late. So I took it in the face, bled into a textbook, waited for the bell to ring.

Queenie was waiting, too, trembling a little, ready to spread my truth. I hoped somehow she'd finish me off. That a bone from my nose would splinter into my brain—I saw that in a movie once—and save me. No such luck.

"WHAT YOU REMEMBER ABOUT your first fuck is how she looks from behind"—this from my older brother, of all people.

Everything in the world that mattered to me was shoved between the last bell and the sound of my mother's car in the garage. After school: door closed, tall girl in my bed, bubble-gum pop drifting up from tinny computer speakers. I'd hear Mom's keys in the bowl by the door, her heels kicked off one by one. By then we would have pulled apart, killed the music, thrown the door open. Maybe we'd spread out some algebra to make it look official.

But my brother was on to us. One night, Mom snoring in front of the television, he crossed my path in the kitchen. The look on his face said he knew everything about me. "Girls," he said, a single commonality after years of silent indifference.

I went to cover my tracks, make something up. "I'm not, you know, like that," I tried.

He was faster. He pounced, poured on the advice. I took it for locker-room talk. I let him go well beyond bounds. Turns out he was right about what you remember, but for the wrong reasons.

SHE LET ME TAKE her picture early on. "Don't get my face in it" was what she said. I'm not proud of how it turned out. I bleached her with the flash, cropped out the cute. What was left could have been anyone.

She made me delete the digital, but I kept a print. I showed it to my new friends—the nerdy squad of boys I clung to in her wake. I shoved it in their faces, stunned them before they could say no, not that they would have. I told them what I remembered about her body, which was everything. I turned our love into a crass play-by-play. I wanted to be seen as an educator to the sexless, a legend among chess players and asthmatics. I could not believe the person she had forced me to become.

"I WOULD TELL YOU if I was," I said to my mom, my heart knocking, after somebody keyed the word into my locker and school made me call her. "I don't have anything against those types of people," I hissed into the phone. "I'm just not, you know, that way."

In the pause I could hear Mom's coworkers, other tele-marketers, making their pleas around her. She slurped something hot. "Rumors," she said then, relieved. "Cliques and bitches—you don't have to explain."

I WAS HAND SHY, in no rush to ruin things with my tall, tall friend. She's the one who made a move. She made us happen. We'd gone glow bowling, which is a thing kids do in this shitbox town. At the Gutter on Friday nights, they turn on black lights, and this fluorescent world shows up. Stickers shaped like stars and sea creatures cover the tiled ceiling. Graffiti—some of it practiced, most just whorled nonsense—sprays all down the lanes. Even the balls are glazed with a luminous resin, unseen in natural light.

Everybody is hideous under those bulbs, all orthodontics and ready whiteheads. That's kind of the point. Nobody is self-conscious. You can relax enough to stop worrying about what the other kids might be thinking. You can focus on knocking down pins or, if you're me, whatever lucky thing might happen to you in the dark.

SHE GOT TWITCHY AFTER a certain ball went into a certain hoop. After the alleged angels. Everything changed when the spirit entered her, she claimed.

She wanted all trace of us gone, she said, eyeing my camera. What's worse, there were other photographers, she confessed. Before me. "Call me sinner," she said, chipper. "Saved by grace!"

Also, she wanted her necklace back, my puka-shell pride. She asked, was I the one who had her lace bralette? Her silver-plated Zippo? I wasn't. I didn't ask what a bralette was. She'd had a life before me, one that included complicated lingerie. And what else? Smoking? Arson? I didn't want to know. She was moving down her long, long list, and could I please return what was rightfully hers?

"Have a blessed day," she told anyone who would listen. She was cultish, cut all her hair off at her coach's request. Something about peripheral vision. From what I could tell, she had very little talent. Clear sight or no, you take enough shots and one is bound to tip in.

MY BROTHER TOLD ME every girl who gives in has been worn down by some other dude. His screeds were turning tedious. "To the dudes who came before," he'd say, tapping my glass with his.

"We're not buddies," I finally told him. Mom had just rushed off to work, and this was breakfast. We were drinking OJ, not beer.

"Tell me everything," he said.

"Too early," I said.

SHE WAS A PRETENDER—a stack of old yearbooks confirmed my suspicions. Before I met her, she'd been a soloist in show choir, knees locked onstage, a semicircle of matching taffeta girls at her back. She'd been a lifeguard and a mathlete, a goth with blond roots. At one point, she'd spearheaded some kind of toothbrush-recycling program.

There was a full-page spread from a homecoming game, my girl cheering front and center in a pink cowboy hat. That one hurt. Our shared hatred of football and country music was a lodestar in this football-and-country-music town—it was how we first found each other. The guy posed next to her had a crew cut and dusty boots, a fat pinch of dip in his cheek.

I scanned her face. Her consistently cocked eyebrow, her unmistakable half smile. Had Crew Cut swayed her with a crossover hit back then, something with an electric banjo and a dance beat? Or was she cowgirl at her core? Did she even *have* a core? Did those awful roper jeans even have back pockets? I couldn't tell.

I jumped around in time. In junior high she'd had ice-blue contact lenses and an asymmetrical haircut. She'd once worn nude lipstick and what I'm pretty sure was a push-up bra. As recently as last semester she'd been way into origami.

NOT MANY PEOPLE KNOW this, but if you complain enough, you can take bowling in place of PE. It helps if you're a weirdo, if the other girls have also complained about dressing in front of you, if your mom has called a meeting with your guidance counselor. If, in what is either the most hilarious or the most embarrassing moment of your life, your mom waggles her tongue between her spread fingers, makes

a kind of "lalala" sound when she does it, a demonstra-
tion of the daily mockery you face. You get the principal's
approval so long as you join a community league. You pick
the Unholy Rollers for the name alone. They are mostly
retirees and widowers, a nice enough bunch. They give you
a shirt with your initials, a little book to keep track of your
scores. Soon you're doing well, making strides. You earn
the nickname "Striker." League night becomes a bright
spot in your miserable semester. You convince yourself that
it's all been worth it. While the other girls are running laps,
you get to sit in the coach's air-conditioned office. You read
about spinners and crankers, skid-snap and rev rates.

WHERE SHE GOES, I follow, even now. Mornings, she sprints
off for practice in the dark, before the dew starts. I crunch
along in the road behind her, keep her haloed in my head-
lights. What she looks like from behind: poised, confident.
She'll glance back and give a low wave. Sometimes she'll
slow to a jog and toss her little sermon through my open
window.

"Turn yourself over to Him," she says. She keeps one
headphone in, won't look at my face. I wait for the mask
to slip, for her to give me some sign that she's still in there.

"Give in gracefully," she says. "Sink like a stone." Something like that. A coin in a well, a corpse in a riptide. *Stop
following me with your car, asshole,* is what she means. "He
knows all," she says, eyebrow cocked. "Every hair on your
head." I take that for a threat.

———

THE CROWD WENT: "GREEN! Green! Green! Green! White-white-white-white-white-white-white!"

One point. Big deal. We lost the game anyway. Killed by the Cougarettes. Mauled, whatever. She poured a lot of Gatorade that night. Rubbed a lot of shoulders. Her team—those girls forgive her everything.

MY BROTHER MUST HAVE heard me bawling from the hallway.

"Why are your blinds closed?" he said as he pushed through my door. He stepped on my bowling shoes, kicked my backpack out of his path. He switched off the sad-bastard ballad I had on repeat. "I'm turning on this lamp," he said. He burped, swiped a pile of my clothes to the floor, sat close to me on the bed. This is how he treats every single room in his life.

He looked at me with a grim smile, waited for an invitation to impart his considerable knowledge. He also wanted me to notice his hair, which I'd noticed right away. It was coated with bleach, raked into frosty swirls. Mom had picked the lemony drugstore shade for herself but hadn't yet worked up the courage to use it. Now it was off-gassing on my brother's head, wretched chemicals wafting.

"Don't cry," he said.

I ignored him, and he sighed in exaggerated pity, patted my feet through the covers.

"Don't be weird," I said. I kicked his hands away and

turned on my side, burritoed the sheet behind me. "Get out."

"Question," he said. "Did you turn out to be, you know, not her type?"

"Out," I said.

"Knew it," he said. He dropped his voice, though Mom wasn't home yet, wouldn't be until the telemarketers had finished their Bud Lights, mangled a bassinet of happy hour mozzarella sticks. "You think she always felt like something was . . . missing?"

"Seriously," I said. "Go."

"I sensed that about her," he said, "that she needs a . . . deep connection."

I tried to be blankets. Dirty clothes in a heap.

"Dick," he said, done with subtlety. "She needs dick.

"But let me tell you something else," he said. "This would have happened anyway, even without . . ." He gestured vaguely at the lump of me, my entire self. "This is just how they do. They get sick of you, and they glom on to the next guy." He whispered "glom" like it was a bodily fluid or an STD. "When they're done with you, they're done."

"You've been a tremendous help," I said. "Now get the fuck out."

He walked over to my desk. He'd gotten bleach all over his T-shirt. Jesus Christ, he'd done his eyebrows, too. They fizzed orange. "Don't take rejection personally," he said.

"Asshole," I said. A slug of snot crept down my cheek and onto the pillow. "There is literally no other way to take it."

He was as tall as he'd ever be, on his way to becoming a spirited little chauvinist. Another short guy bursting with insight. "I'm trying to help you," he said. I felt sorry for him then. It hadn't happened yet, but one day some girl would split his heart, bleed him like a pig.

He sat in my desk chair, took a sloppy sip from my water bottle. He pulled out drawers, fumbled around. This was the real reason he'd come into my room. Her picture.

"It's not in there," I said.

"Just show me," he said. "Now that it's over."

He unzipped my camera bag and peeked at nothing. He closed the drawers, ran his fingers along the underside of the desk.

"Not even warm," I said.

He knocked my graphing calculator onto the floor. Map pencils rolled.

"Show me that puss," he whined. "You've shown every-body else."

I could smell his scorched head. Underneath the froth, his curls mottled blond.

"You look like you should be giving truck-stop hand jobs with that hair," I said.

He flipped through the pages of my notebook, posed with a pencil in his hand like he was ready to sketch a sus-pect.

"At least tell me who she dumped you for," he said.

"Blow jobs," I said. "All the jobs."

"Who's the dude?" he said. "Somebody good-looking? Popular?"

"You have no idea," I said.

He picked up a protractor and used it to poke at his raw scalp.

"Shit burns," he said.

"ARE YOU SURE I'M not too tight?" she used to ask. As if such a thing were possible. As if she could be too pink, too sweet. It was a question meant to haunt. The type of thing straight girls teach other straight girls to say. I talk to her now, and she stares off at some point beyond me. She's the worst kind of ghost—breathing, wearing wind shorts. Born again. She hands out flyers for the Chastity Club, wears a homemade T-shirt that says "WAIT" in pastel puff paint. She is all teeth and faith, terrifying in her happiness.

I don't have to look far to see the kind of woman she'll become—this town is bloated with them. Women who met their soul mate in youth group and got married young. Mission trips and the missionary position and grace before every meal. It's a life of pew PDA with the hubby, clapping on the downbeat, hating the sin, not the sinner. Hair spray, potlucks, half a dozen kids. A big, fat scrapbooking habit.

Like that, but with basketball.

MOM HAS A JESUS fish decal on the back of our car just like everybody else, but we stopped going to services. She pretends this decision is something she hasn't thought about much.

She soaks her feet on Sunday mornings, pulls apart the newspaper. In the afternoons, I drive us to the Gutter, where there's a two-for-one special. It's me against me. Mom sits in the molded plastic chairs, painting her nails or reading her magazines, hooting for my strikes. "Day of rest," she says. "That's what I believe in."

Or maybe I'm wrong about my girl. Maybe one day in some distant future, when she finally lands on an identity— a health nut? a hoarder?—she'll look back on these shape-shifting years and crack up. *Oh my God,* she'll say to herself, her authentic self, the real person she's become. *Show choir!* she'll scream. *Basketball! Remember when I wore those creepy fucking contact lenses? Remember when I was gay for, like, a minute?*

On bad days, my future is too clear. It has bowling, crushing loneliness.

On good days, I tell myself this lie: She was *my* phase.

I FINALLY SHOWED HER picture to my brother—flipped it up over the cereal box and into his lap one morning.

"Pussssss" was what he said.

He turned it sideways. He stared at it for some time. "I've seen better," he said at last, pocketing the thing.

FIDDLEBACKS

THIS HOUSE IS A HOUSE where you shake out your shoes. We have bloodsuckers, creepy-crawlies. If it's pissed off and fits in a boot, we've got it. Conenoses and masked hunters, lone star ticks and brown dog ticks. We have scorpions. *Scorpions.* Bull's-eye bugs, my brother calls them. Bugs that put you in a wheelchair or make it so one side of your face droops for always. They're sprung and ready, waiting to strike at your dark toe.

We keep our boots set heel to heel in the mudroom, Mother's orders. We do guesswork on socked walks down the stairs. It's gotten to be a competition now.

We all want to escape something spectacular, but it's my brother who gets the best crawlers. By best I mean worst.

I don't scream anymore, but sometimes I still get the shivers.

My brother, he's fearless, and he keeps track. He tosses the horrible ones into a glass jar with spiked cotton. He kills them enough to get a pin through, labels them with the tiniest block letters you've ever seen. That folded foam board, his pride. "Hurts me more than it hurts them," he says. "But"—he nods—"science." The legs keep on moving until they stop.

This setup works double time to spite Sis, who is worse, my brother says, than a gee-dee fisherman. She swears she tipped a silver-beaked assassin once when nobody but her was there to see it whole. She kicked a quick foot at us that day, said, "I'm lucky I'm alive." What she showed off was mostly smeared and so mushed together with her pink sock you couldn't tell much about it. My brother and I squinted at what was left on the floor. I'm no expert, but I couldn't see any beak in the mix.

"Bullcrap," my brother spat at Sis. "No assassins around here. Longitude, among other known facts." He forced a no-smash pact and made us do our handshake. Now we tap-tap shoe by shoe when he is there to interpret what scuttles out. You don't mess with my brother's bugs.

Sunday mornings, our house is ours alone. Mother catches a ride to the early service, leaves with wet hair and nothing fixed for us to eat. We pit stop at the pantry, make do with dry spaghetti we lick and dip into the sugar sack.

In the mudroom, my brother sets up his jar at the threshold. He uses a dish towel to rub at his magnifying glass. It's ladies first.

"Left foot," he bosses.

I turn a June bug and Sis turns a June bug. They crawl in a clump on the floor until my brother crunches them. If there is one thing our board has enough of, it's June bugs.

My brother clears his throat. He shakes out his shoulders, makes a bridge with his fingers to pop every knuckle. He picks up the boot and holds it high over his head like it's the Jesus cup and we're the ones at church. "Get on with it," Sis says.

He's tipping slow, slow, and then all at once it's over. We know before the thing hits the floor that we've lost. My brother has topped us with a giant stag, the king of beetles. It's harmless but horned, blue black, and glittering. "Who's my rascal?" he says, letting it crawl all over. "Who's my big boy?" He puts it on his head, spins around in circles, does a little do-si-do all by himself. He whispers something only the beetle can hear and drops it in the jar.

"Big shit," Sis says, "when you have boats like those." It's true that my brother is all boot. When he wears them, you can push your thumb anywhere a toe should be and feel nothing pushing back.

"You're a triple socker," Sis says to him. "You're a fake."

"Secondhanded," my brother says. "Circumstances extenuated."

Mother says better too loose than too tight. It's the golden rule of thrifting. My brother flaps around like empty clothes on a line, his pearl-snap shirt to his knees and those baggy blue jeans. He doesn't mind a little room, he says. He's trying to trigger a growth spurt.

Our right feet are a bust—a clot of roly-polys and a stuck-together Band-Aid. Nothing worth tacking, my brother says. "Let's hunt."

He has another jar for keeping, not killing. It's cozy, holes punched in the top and a bed of sand at the bottom, a frogman from the fish tank for company. When we go looking, my brother holds this jar out front, level as a lantern. He has fiddleback hopes. It's eating him up—all he can talk about. He wants to set one loose in some poor bastard's mailbox.

STUBBS IS UNDER OUR Wrangler, just legs sticking out. The long block has been knocking, he says, and he is changing the oil, too. Stubbs is like this, Mother says. He goes down once and does it all. Old oil rainbows our drive. My brother doesn't know about long blocks, but he doesn't want to learn from Stubbs. Sis and I don't want to hand Stubbs the plus screwdriver or the minus screwdriver or the tools we have no way to tell apart. Stubbs is the type that, when you're walking with him, will put his hand on the back of your neck to steer you.

We leap over the legs on tiptoe, quiet and fast like when we play hell over the space between our two couches. Stubbs says, "Hey, strangers," from under our truck because we aren't fast enough or quiet enough and our house sits in a way where there's no place to go but straight out.

"Got a hand?" Stubbs says.

Stubbs under a truck is his best first impression. So much is wrong with his face, you don't know where it is you should be looking. The trouble starts at the nose and goes neckward.

"He's getting a lot closer to what he was," Mother always tells us. "Doctors work miracles these days."

The proof is in a snapshot he keeps taped to his dashboard—a young Stubbs posed on the hood of a hot rod, facing the camera full on. Stubbs is so brave, Mother says, a real work in progress. My brother says we'll have to take her word. He says we won't be riding around with Stubbs anytime soon, that if he had been a better driver, maybe he wouldn't have flipped his IROC and turned his-self into a monster. The closest I ever saw Mother get to popping my brother in the mouth was when he wondered, "How come somebody that butt ugly isn't rich or smart or not boring as hell to cancel it all out?"

"God's plan" is what Mother said when she was finished being furious.

"That stuff coming out the tailpipe weren't water." This is Stubbs, still talking. If he makes it past noticing whatever is right in front of him, he'll start in on the weather—or worse, school.

Our best bet is to get out of earshot, hightail to make the legs and the Wrangler and our house into very small things. We sprint until we're nowhere, past our neighbor's neighbor's plot. It's just highway and pasture dotted with buzz-cut alpacas, skinny and scabbed around the ears. Sis starts in with her cartwheels all in a row like magic, her yellow hair fanning out. I know less and less about what she's thinking, why she still does some things the same as she always has and why she scrunches up her dumb face at others. She's always telling jokes my brother and I don't get— insults we can reckon only by the stupid lilt in her voice. She looks for her reflection everywhere, when there's a mirror or plate glass around she'll stop everything and tilt her chin so it catches the light. If my brother or I accidentally walk in on her in the bathroom, she screams like we've lit her on fire, but it's always just her standing around in Mother's bathrobe with her face scrubbed red, doing nothing at all. Once we three took baths together, the water rust orange and flecked with our dirt, Sis the one in front who made sure nobody got scalded.

My brother is picking apart bug song—telling us which is cicada and which is katydid. On down the road, too far for us to see, is town. Town is the church with Mother in it, our school, and not much else.

Sis gets a stitch in her side and stops to find the kind of rock that makes stitches go away. She toes road trash while my brother and I stand around not helping. The trick to a stitch rock is that only the person who's hurting knows which type will work.

Our heat is the kind that catches up and straddles you.

Standing still is when you start to sweat. Sis is taking her sweet time, bending at the waist when the big rigs go by, priding herself on the horns that blow. "That's another one," she says, dust spraying out as a Walmart transporter flies by. This is something she keeps track of, to show how special she thinks she is. Truckers honk for me only when I give them a double thumbs-up or wave really big with both hands. My brother is always too busy with whatever bug to notice who might be ripping through this place.

Now Sis has her T-shirt bikinied, the bottom pulled up through its own neck hole. My brother looks at her, looks away, and hocks a glob on the asphalt. He tells us now is no time to forget about the fiddleback. "Kill two birds," he says to Sis. He says spiders seek shade, same as we do.

Sis uses her long legs to put quick space between us. She tries to look like she's out here alone, like it's this big coincidence and we're just some kids who happen to look exactly like her, only shorter. She cocks her hip and shades her eyes to stare into every car that blows through. She is humming her secret song—no point in even asking what it is—smiling her private smile.

My brother lets me hold the special jar for a while. Believe me, the fields are nothing but loopers and bagworms and boll weevils, but this doesn't stop my brother from turning me down a row of cotton that doesn't belong to us.

"You're evens," he says, and sets out for odds.

Our sun is so bright you can't tell apart the real-world grit from what's floating on the backside of your eyeball.

The heat gets you crazed. You walk around with the word "modicum" on repeat in your mind. It's a word my brother taught me.

Walking a row over, my brother is in love with the sound of his own self. He is off, spinning out. It's a little-known fact, he says, that spiders move their legs with blood pressure and muscle both. Did I know that in spiders the number of eyes range from zero to eight?

"For example," my brother says. "Case in point," he says.

He is tromping on our neighbor's plants, dreaming out loud. When he gets a fiddleback, he will name it Lucifer, Jr., or Mr. Kill. He will feed it lard with his fingers. He will fatten it up, and when the time is right, he will pick a stranger from the white pages. "It's the perfect crime," he says. Nobody my brother doesn't know is safe.

SIS STILL HAS HER stitch when we start back empty-handed. We are sticky, the tops of our ears pink and crisp. "It's triple digits," she guesses. It's time to head home or fall down crying.

My brother points to thunderheads Sis and I can't see. "We'll try again tomorrow," he says, "when it's cooler and when the rain has flushed out even the shiest ess-oh-bees."

Sis and I are walking in step, our sweaty arms slapping against each other. She's got a slime to her, thanks to that lotion she wears, but I don't mind it too much. She smells like watermelon and chemicals, not so bad. Some of her glitter gets on me, and I don't mind that, either. I figure this is the closest I'll get to her letting me borrow any.

My brother runs up ahead, then bends down on one knee and whistles low into the burnt grass. "You ladies ever seen a Texas-bred fistface?" he shouts back to us. When I rush over to his cupped hands, he throws nothing in the air and cocks his arm back like to hit me. "My fist, your face," he screams, and dies laughing.

"Didn't even flinch," I say, and it's true. My brother would never hit me, not ever.

"Jackasses," Sis says, and saunters past us both, up to the house. We're used to this. At school she's a traitor, walking faster than my brother and me, leaving us behind at the flagpole so she can bust through the front doors alone.

Stubbs is still legs only—the greased-up guts of our truck spread out in the drive. It's too hot for games. We don't run to jump over the legs, and this time the legs don't ask us for help. On our porch, my brother gets his second wind. He jumps up and dunks Sis's head like he's dunking her underwater. She tries to knock him in the solar plex, but he slips away. "Too quick for chickens," he says, high-stepping into the house, still king.

"IT'S KID DIRT THAT baits them," Mother says. She means the bugs. "What we are," Mother says, "is infested." Church gets her worked up. She has come home at the best or worst time, depending on how you take it. My brother is sticking his stag in two places because it's so huge and so not dead it keeps spinning itself around on the board.

"He's a fighter," my brother says, so proud.

"Mercy," Mother says. "Not in the house." Mother's theory is like draws like.

We've moved our whole operation into the living room because our show is on. I'm in charge of reception. I hold the antennae in one hand and aim my other arm out the window. Every fan in the house is plugged in and pointed just so. Sis has ice chips melting in her bra.

"It's no wonder," Mother says, on her knees, whisking at ants.

The trail of them goes up and over the coffee table. They drown and collect in iced tea rings or sluicing lakes of cola. Some survive to trudge into shag. The strongest make it across my brother's sweaty socks and under the couch where he sits lolling. He pinches one and holds it to the light.

"These," my brother says to Mother, "are nobody's fault." He rolls his fingers together. "These are fire," he explains. "Not sugar. No, ma'am."

He doesn't mention the carpenters in the doorframes or the Texas crazies nested in the wall sockets, eating wires. We have rovers and pharaohs in our potted plants, acrobats with their heart-shaped butts, plus ghosts, my brother's favorite, pale headed and harmless but with a reek like foul coconut if you crush them.

"We live in filth," Mother says. "We're disgusting little piggy people."

Sis turns up the set with her toe. My brother has let her have the best couch, the one with the better view and the butt divot. My brother picks his battles and is busy, besides.

I hear a woman crying, hospital machines bleeping. "Somebody say what's happening," I say. If I make a move to look, the screen goes haywire. Sis sighs her sigh—the same one she uses when she tells some little story or jokey thing that I don't get and I ask her to break it into pieces for me. She's working some fruity gunk into her legs, even creaming her feet, making every part of herself so soft.

Sis says, "When it's commercials."

It's a real-life emergency show about people who have been mangled by machines or who have lost limbs to wild animals or have had both sides of themselves stabbed through. The surgeons are the stars. They have tiny cameras clipped to their masks. There's nothing they won't show on our show.

My brother is copying the stag's genus and species from the *Britannica,* blocking it out in Magic Marker. Mother is on a tear, pointing to potato-chip dust ground down in the carpet, sticky midnight dishes stashed in the laundry basket.

"If you start with the vacuum," my brother says to her, "then I don't know what."

When my arm muscles start to give and the picture is not what it could be, my brother says, "Enough's enough," and puts Sis at the TV.

"Only because I want to," Sis says. "It's cooler standing."

My brother gets up and poots into the box fan, and Sis and I holler and breathe into our hands. He takes Sis's seat, and I take over at the board. His sloping script is hopeless. I trace it over to make a neater job, but I have my work cut out. White froth spews from the stag and makes everything smeary. I remember too late that beetle stink takes forever to get off your hands. Onscreen, there is something bloody and peeled back. It could be a kneecap, or not.

"You hate to see that," the surgeon says, his scalpel a pointer pointing.

"All right," I say. "Tell me what it is I'm looking at."

Mother is mopping herself into a corner, saying, "Out, out, every blessed one!"

She could disinfect us to death and wipe the wood grain off the kitchen table, but terrible things would still squeeze through clefts in the floor. Horrors would come up the sink or else ride in on the dog's back or fly right through the windows we keep cracked to catch the cross-breeze.

WHEN THE SUN GOES down, Stubbs is at the screen door, his cap pulled low and his collar flipped up. Sis is always the first of us to answer a ringing phone or a door that starts knocking. My brother toes the TV off and flips open the *Britannica* quick to make like he has been reading.

Stubbs is shuffling his feet on the porch.

"You need to use the crapper, use the crapper," Sis says to him.

"Can Claris come out?" Stubbs says like that, like Sis is the mother and Mother is the daughter.

"Mom," Sis booms. "It's him."

Mother comes out of the kitchen, drying her hands on her apron. She's the type who wears one just to boil water.

"Stop yelling, you," Mother says. "You see I'm coming."

Stubbs takes off his cap when he sees Mother. The bare porch bulb doesn't do him any favors. When you catch him in the corner of your eye, you're scared somebody masked is coming at you. Mother dusts the front of her blouse and sweeps hair out of her face. Sis keeps to her post at the door. My brother has given up his pretend reading. He and I are chinning the best couch, turned backward to watch.

"Lost my light," Stubbs says. "Finish her up tomorrow."

He sets a dented hodgepodge can down by the door. "Keep these little bits from rusting?" he says. "What's spread out there is tarped."

Stubbs thumbs over his shoulder. "Rain on the way," he says.

"Let me make you a plate," Mother says to Stubbs. She touches the screen with her flat palm.

Stubbs says, "No need."

"Pie?" Mother says. "Coffee?"

"Water's fine," Stubbs says. "Since you're insisting."

Mother turns back for the kitchen.

"Deedra," Mother says, and stares at Sis.

"Claris," Sis says, and rolls her eyes. Mother stares her mother stare until Sis sighs and follows her. The truth is all of us are a little afraid of the things Sis might say. She can turn hot and ugly in an instant, hissing at whoever is standing closest. Keeping her busy is the best thing.

My brother and I watch Stubbs.

"Rain," he says to us, and thumbs over his shoulder again. "Break this drought." Stubbs's face is divvied up. His seams stay white even when the rest gets a suntan.

Sis comes out sullen with the good silver pitcher and a pair of forks. Mother is behind her with a cloudy mug from the freezer and the biggest slice of mud pie you can fit on a plate. She has matches between her teeth.

"Gonna have my one smoke," she says with half her mouth.

"You already had it," my brother says.

Mother pops the screen door open with her hip.

"Last night," she says. "It's last night you're thinking."

"Tonight," my brother says. "Just before."

"Last night," Mother says. Stubbs takes the pitcher and the forks from Sis. He takes the book of matches away from Mother's lips.

"Don't come crying at me when you've got tar lungs," my brother says, and Mother flaps her hand at him, low and quick.

Sis closes the screen door behind Mother and Stubbs. She closes the oak door, too.

"Now we can't see," my brother says.

"Nothing to see," Sis says. "Except him making a mess of that pie."

It's true that Stubbs jaws his food sideways. Sis sits down and pulls on her lip. She is thinking something through, getting mean.

"Let them have their fun," she says, buckshot straight at my brother.

He goes to the window and rips open the drapes.

"I'll do it," I say, and jump up quick. "Read your book." It's easier this way.

I watch Mother and Stubbs set up a lap picnic on our hanging swing. Stubbs cups his hand and lights two cigarettes. He passes one to Mother.

The wind picks up, blowing Mother's hair, streaming it across her face and across Stubbs's face, too.

The crickets cut off.

Our rain starts out silent—the thirsty dirt sucks it in too quick to hear a splash. Then a patter gets going in the cotton plots. It starts to thump on the rusted silo that says the name of our dumb town. It falls on the dusty topsides of our neighbor's slack cattle, turns to a silvery drip in our back-lot ditch. Big slugs pelt heavy on burned-out horse stalls and scattered trash. Then all at once it swarms our house, which is not tin roofed but sure does sound like it.

"Anything to report?" my brother says.

I say, "I'd say if there was." My best thing, if I have one, is knowing when to keep my mouth shut.

Mother and Stubbs, they are porched and dry, watching it come down.

––––––––

RAIN OR NO RAIN, this is a house that heats up at night. The living room is the coolest room, the couches more comfortable than our beds, besides. My brother's sticky feet are in my face, on my pillow, because of how we are staggered. Sis is a furnace—she throws off her swelter when she dreams. Nobody can stand to be near her. Since she doesn't have to share, she gets the worst couch. It's a trade my brother and I can live with.

My brother never stops, even when we are supposed to be sleeping.

"Hard to find the fiddle right after they molt," he says. "That's a fact."

"Hmm," I say. It's that time before sleep when my brother's ideas get further and further apart and all of us start emptying out, breathing together in the same slow way.

"If there's a trick to the recluse," he says in the dark.

When the highway is wet, even all the way out here, you can make out the steady black-slush sound that comes off the semis.

"Maybe the trick is to find out what they want. Set a trap. Bees to honey," he says.

A flash cracks white, and we all pop up. I am counting Mississippis, and nobody is saying anything, so I think my brother and Sis must be counting them, too. When the rumble comes, loud but far away, I stop holding my breath.

"Idiot," Sis says. She throws her pillow at my brother's head. "Bees to honey. Why don't you go catch a cow with milk?"

Mother comes out into the hollow dark of the hall.

"Mercy!" she says. "We're electrified."

She walks to the window and parts the curtains, lets some moonlight spill onto her hands and face. She says, "To farmers rain sounds like money falling." Her hair is wrapped up neat in her scarf. It's too dark to see, but you can bet she has her makeup off and her wrinkle grease on. She is tiny in her pajama set, tiny standing in the shadowed living room. The only time Mother can be still is when it's too dark for her to see our messes that need cleaning.

She closes the curtains, comes to each of us, and nuzzles our heads. "How are my littles?" she says, and we pretend to push her away. She leaves her smell all over us. Mothers, they can tell their children apart. Even in blind dark, she knows who's who.

Mother gets under the covers with Sis like she's one of us, one of the kids.

She used to pester on Sunday mornings, yank the sheets back, threaten us with pots and pans and thrown water. She was lavender soap and hair spray, hovering by our beds.

"Don't make me," she would say. "Don't think I won't do it."

But Mother did not, not ever. Instead she made a big show of clomping around in her Jesus heels, slapping at us through the blankets, but soft like we were little babies and Mother was some mother trying to get her babies to burp.

She's snoring, gone in an instant, always so tired. I can

feel my brother restless and awake with his spider thoughts, but Sis is starting to dissolve, too. We can always tell she's out by the way her legs start to twitch. Sometimes she'll thrash a little and make these deep, throaty noises we never hear from her in the daytime. My brother says it's nightmare demons chasing her, that she's getting payback for being so nasty every waking minute, but that's not what it sounds like. There's happy mixed into those moans, something sweet. I think part of her must be off doing something that feels good, like maybe she's turning cartwheels or eating candy in some other world, some place where my brother and I aren't allowed.

"Hey," he'll bark if she starts with her sounds. "Quit it."

I always tell him it's fine, that it doesn't bother me, but he leans over and shakes her shoulder every time, tugs her back from wherever she's gone.

"Bothers me," he'll say. "Nobody needs to hear that."

"THAT THEM?" MY BROTHER asks. It isn't.

Mother and Stubbs are catching the late show. We have done the movie math, accounted for the previews, the credits even. Mother is late, out in this weather.

"Then what are you looking at?" my brother wants to know.

"Flyers are out," I say, peeling back the drapes and pointing.

The rain has not stopped all week—the drought busted

wide open. Our Wrangler is still tarped, my brother's fiddle-back still running free. Winged things have come in from the wet. They press themselves against our house or spread out flat under the eaves.

"Anything worth a gee-dee?" my brother asks. He has a lip print from mother's bird peck on his cheek. We all do. He doesn't look up from the set, where a man is gurneyed and snakebit.

"Moths," I say. Powdery skippers and flashers, looks like. Nothing we haven't already got. They bat against the windows and beat around the porch lights. I'm on watch for sicklewings, my brother tells me, but I'm not sure what to look for.

"Yell if you spot purple," he says.

Then it's the local news—a fire put out and a forecast for more rain. Sis paints her toenails red, and my brother says she'll kill us all, breathing that poison. Then we three are squished on the good couch and it's a grown-up movie, like the one Mother and Stubbs went to see but with all the grown-up parts cut out. We stop watching because there's not enough left to make sense of. Every light in our house is lit.

My brother gets up to pull the drapes apart.

"He drives like hell," my brother says. "You've seen the dust he kicks up."

"No dust to kick tonight," Sis says. Our land is churned-up mud, black pools knee-deep.

"Fiddlebacks," my brother says. "I'm going out."

"In this?" Sis says. "You're an idiot."

"I'm waterproof," my brother says. Sis stands next to my brother and looks outside.

"Y'all can come if y'all want to," he says. Sometimes he talks so big.

"Let's take a vote," I say.

"I vote no vote," he says, and that's that.

I don't know why Sis decides to come along, but I know why I do. It's because my brother takes my hand. He is such a good talker, the kind of person who makes you believe you can be led someplace better.

So we're running to the mudroom like it's the most natural thing for us to do, to go outside in the deepest worst of night, wearing trash bags with holes slit out for our heads. We do a quick boot tip—a silverfish for my brother, zero for Sis and me—and then we are out in the drench, flashlighting our way down the drive. My brother has his special jar armpitted under his Hefty bag. He tells us to train our eyes for small things.

"They'll tend away from the beam," he says. "Watch for what's running."

The tarped Wrangler looks and sounds like a nightmare, furious and flapping behind us in the dark. There is no path we can take away from it, so we stomp straight through the muck. The drizzle comes at us sideways, pinpricking our faces.

"You should be looking down," my brother says to Sis and me. "Why aren't you looking down?"

There is never much to do out here, and there is even less to do now, in the pitch-black wet. We go to the side of our house where there is our pile of junk. Some of the mess is made up of things that used to be ours. Some of it is trash that belongs to nobody, and some of it comes from strangers passing through—drivers losing their sunglasses or hats to the wind. I see sunglasses and hats. I see a jumbo roll of carnival tickets and a dinner plate with a woodpecker painted on it. There is Mother's old housecoat in the heap.

My brother shakes loose a tangled water hose, flips up a flattened kiddie pool. It seems to me he is kicking things for kicking's sake.

"You know to always be looking for eggs, right?" my brother says to Sis and me.

"Cottony," he says. "Like mold but white." He has to shout over rushing water and the squish-suck of our boots in mud. "Eggs is the best-case scenario."

We are soaked through, shivering.

"Asinine," Sis says. "Spider hunting in a monsoon."

IT IS MY BEAM that catches Stubbs's parked car, pulled off on the side of our house like that. For so long I have been looking for tiny things running—the car seems bigger than a car should be, and Mother and Stubbs seem bigger than two people inside it.

"Here they are," I say, like it is Mother and Stubbs we have been looking for. At first there's not much I can make out about what's happening in the car. Then I can. I let my flashlight fall. The pelt dampens and nobody hears me.

Only Sis is too close behind. Her ray replaces mine, on Stubbs's car, on Stubbs and Mother inside. I see my same thoughts cross her wet face. The windows are fogged, steamy but still see-through: the back of Mother's head a nest, snarled. Stubbs's stitched face straining. Their pairs of locked legs.

The car is moving up and down, squeak-squeak. I think of the thing I heard Sis say once about not knocking when something is rocking. There's a slick foot on the windshield, sliding. I can't swallow. I look at Sis for help, but her face has changed. Her thoughts are not my thoughts, not any-more. There isn't a tangle of fear and shame twisting inside her. She's not afraid; she's curious, her face flushed red with want. I've been looking at the wrong things. Soon Sis will be gone, too, steaming up a different car with a different Stubbs, my brother and me outside it.

She shines her light at me, at my face.

Our brother, he has fallen behind, but he is coming now and coming fast, his flashlight aimed low at the sodden ground, seconds away from what he already knows.

STARLITE

THERE'S ANOTHER WORLD UNDERNEATH THIS one, easy enough to get to. "It's like we're lifting the—what is it?" Jill said. "Is 'scrim' a word?" You could slip right out of your life.

It had been a while since she'd done this much. Things had gotten to the point where every statement she made seemed to clamor for a corresponding movement. She snatched frantic little handfuls of nothing from the air. Rick sat on the bed watching. She was in her bra and underwear, a matching set she'd picked out for the occasion, and though she was very high, she was still aware of Rick's eyes on her body. She bent over in front of him, at the waist, of course, the way every girl in the history of sex has been taught to bend. With both hands, she pulled something invisible off the revolting carpet, lifted it up and over her head. Maybe the motions were stupid, but she couldn't keep herself from making them. She hoped she was coming across as an erotic mime, a sexy interpreter for the deaf.

"Scrim's a word," he said. He was smiling, staring at her ass.

"Well," Jill said, her hands made into claws. "This is us, ripping through it."

Rick was bigger than Jill's husband. This difference was crucial to her, and she had imagined him with a furry chest, something she might rub with lotion, work up into a good froth. At work, in his button-down shirts and corduroy jackets, everything about Rick suggested he was burly. The beard, for example, and the knuckles sprouted with red hair. She was disappointed, after he'd tossed off his shirt, to see such creamy smoothness, such even tone. Still, he had the barrel chest, the thick arms that made her feel tiny and perfect. Her husband was wiry and fit, meticulously groomed.

Jill had insisted on something seedy, so they were in a place off Westheimer you could rent by the hour. She'd driven past it a thousand times and had always felt a tug—the garish lavender stucco was a pathetic attempt at tropical, the word "Vacancy" was trapped in a blinking white star. It was hard to believe their office building was so close—the zoning laws in Houston were batshit—they could have walked over, not that they would have. She'd parked her new Infiniti next to Rick's older Infiniti, and they'd both double-beeped their car alarms. Not far from the parking lot was a plasma donation center, but also the galleria and a string of glass-fronted boutiques. One shop sold only home theater equipment, another specialized in bespoke chinos—luxuries not meant for the guests who usually stayed here. Even the word "guests" felt wrong to Jill. Customers, maybe. Frequenters. This place was rock bottom for anybody, a good spot for bad decisions.

"There are only two things people do in places like this," Rick said. "And we've already done all the drugs."

"Funny," Jill said. She wasn't going to let him fuck her. Probably not.

She riffed through a series of calisthenics, ridiculous leg lifts and lunges. Speeding.

Rick was only kidding—of course there were more drugs. There were the two baggies he knew she had seen, plus the one she knew he was keeping to surprise her with later. Plus there was the one he thought she didn't know about.

"You be the executor," she'd told him. She didn't like to hold on to it.

They didn't smoke in real life, but in this room they did. Rick brought fancy clove cigarettes that sizzled and snapped and tasted like Christmas. They lit them one after the other, waved them around like sparklers. He'd brought cupcakes with sprinkles, the jumbo kind, and fast food, too, warm burgers in a greasy paper bag. Two large cups of orange soda, a mess of fries. Who could eat under such circumstances?

Rick could. He sat on the bed in his boxer shorts, fries falling into his lap, smiling at her. He always seemed so sober. "I do this a lot more than you do" was his excuse.

The music she'd chosen was playing over the little speakers he had brought. She'd spent weeks planning the soundtrack, mapping out the pace, timing the transitions just so. Like any good mix, it started with familiar and then ramped up to the weird. She'd worked in B-sides and bizarre covers and the truly absurd—there were throat singers and a band that used a dot matrix printer as a drum machine—gems she was certain Rick hadn't heard before. A playlist is always an act of exhibition, but more important, Jill wanted to orchestrate her high. She'd anchored the day with artful repetitions and themes, refrains that would energize for hours and then, she hoped, bring her down easy. She wanted songs she could listen to later, back in the real world, that would trigger a feeling like something in her bloodstream.

At work, Jill and Rick spoke in code, acted like children. They called Rick's wife Eyelash and Jill's husband Kneecap, the genesis of the names long forgotten, a product of some drunken happy hour. Rick drew eyes on a staple remover and they named it Sharkey. Passed back and forth between their cubicles, it was a running gag, where the little guy would turn up—jammed into Jill's box of tissues, once submerged in Rick's cup of coffee.

"I knew you'd get nekkid today," Rick said, and bit into a burger.

"I'm not!" she said, but naked might be on the table. It wasn't even nine a.m.

Rick had taken a vacation day, and Jill called out sick. He was her supervisor, so it was his voicemail that she called. She left the message from the motel room, right in front of him, breathless and giggling while he watched. They wondered if people at work would raise their eyebrows at the two of them missing. They hoped so.

He licked salt from his fingers and watched her. "How do you like this?" Jill said. She was fanning her arms out, bending at the elbows.

"It's a little air traffic control–y," Rick said.

She should have eaten something, but now it was too late. Food was ruined.

She sat on the floor, scissored her legs. "Pay attention," Jill said. "These are moves from the future."

EVERYWHERE JILL LOOKED, THINGS were interesting. In the strange, scrimless world of the motel room, each object had a fascinating, dingy significance: the obscure fire escape map mounted to the inside of the door, the golden light slicing beneath it. The plastic alarm clock by the bed flashed midnight, the snooze bar covered in whorled fingerprints.

"That time's wrong, you know," Jill said.

Rick said, "Thanks, Einstein."

She flipped him off and smiled, checked her watch again. It was an antique, a dead person's accessory ticking on. It was a recent gift from her husband, ornate but delicate, surprisingly light on the wrist. *Good Kneecap,* she thought. He'd had her initials engraved on the back, that last letter another thing he'd given her. She conjured time backward, an ancestral stream of Kneecaps: men who looked like her husband but with weird hats or wild hair, one guy sitting on a throne, some sullen kid at the edge of the wilderness, frowning at a fresh kill.

She went into a deep lunge and came up. She looked at her pretty watch again, picked up her phone. No calls, no texts—good, nothing to pull at her. Everything she looked at was framed, fringed by her human self. Why didn't she always notice this? She admired her hand, how it held her phone in the air, then the lovely arm leading up to the hand that held the phone. She took so much for granted every day. The hinge in her elbow was a wonderful thing—her entire body was conveniently covered with skin. Around the edges of her vision hung the lace of her hair, and just beyond that, Rick was at her side, adorable and breathing, also covered in skin.

They smoked and ashed, smoked and ashed. Jill showed Rick the time on her wrist, and they marveled at how early it was, their coworkers just getting to the office, pouring their coffee and starting their day. She felt her human thigh against Rick's human thigh, and it was so nice to be in this place, warm and alive, away from her computer and her paper shredder, the multi-line telephone and crushing boredom. Sitting still was impossible, though, meaningful thigh connection or not. She jolted up and did another set of jumping jacks, put her hand over her racing heart. She checked her watch. "Still early," she said, and Rick laughed.

"Still midnight," he said.

"It's fun now," Jill said, "but it's gonna get so bad."

A song they loved came from the little speakers, and they swooned, singing along. Rick had a sweet voice, high and pure, a deep Southern lilt. Jill had worked hard to get rid of her own accent, mimicking anchorwomen and soap stars since she was small. Rick was from a little town in Arklatexhoma—maybe the quadruple influence of all those slow vowels was too much for him to get out from under. Anyway, Jill liked the way they sounded coming from him.

She danced, looking at herself in the mirror. Rick could dance, too, very well, as she recalled from the holiday party, though now he stayed moored to the bed, smoking, watching her.

"This playlist is a masterpiece," he said. "Your taste is—" He brought his fingers to his mouth and kissed them.

"I know," she said.

"Seriously," he said. "I keep waiting for it to suck."

"It won't," Jill said. "It makes me fall in love with myself."

They'd determined long ago that Eyelash and Kneecap had similar, terrible taste in music.

"More?" she said. They were using a key, trying to make it last. They took turns, and another song came on. They swooned again. It was a British band, a group who toyed with dissonance and celestial chords.

"See?" he said. "I can't believe you know this one—you're too young!"

She said, "I'm telling you."

"I saw them play up in Denton when you were probably still in diapers," he said. "They just stood around looking half-dead and depressed, completely annoyed by the audience. It was spectacular."

"I wish I'd been there," Jill said. "I've seen the live stuff online, but it's not the same."

Rick said she was an old soul, and Jill said, "Fuck you." She countered that she had the youngest of souls—tight, pretty, and pink. She danced into the bathroom and turned on the water in the tub.

The bathroom was its own humid ecosystem—gnats floated near the sink, and it felt much hotter than the rest of the room. Like the stucco outside, the walls were painted a loud, streaky purple, but the trim and linoleum were light green. The door was swollen and waterlogged and hard to close, not that Jill wanted to close it. She swung it back and forth to the beat. Even the knob had been painted over, moist and grainy to the touch. The latch was busted—somebody trying to get out or get in, Jill couldn't decide—the wood splintered and nude, mint-colored chips swept into a dim corner. She danced over to the toilet, lifted the lid, and peeked inside. It smelled terrible in the expected ways, but more interesting was a syrupy top note—vomit, probably—which combined with the bizarre paint job to make Jill feel nauseous but also giddy, like she was stuck inside a rotten piece of taffy. It was all exactly as she'd hoped. She danced back to the tub.

"I'm gonna wash-wash-wash-wash-wash my feet," she sang over the storming water. She sat on the grimy porcelain lip and messed with the hot and cold taps. Then Rick was leaning in the doorway, filling it with his size, watching while she used a cracked gray bar of soap to lather her skinny toes.

She turned off the water, splashed her legs around in the tub. Images came to her in full color, perfect little flashes, buzzing and glorious: her husband spinning a tennis racket in his hands; the heart-shaped night-light she'd had in her childhood bedroom; an animal running through a field of high fire. There was an impossibly long, kinked hair clinging to the tile wall. Jill looped and looped it with her ring finger. It belonged to someone beautiful, she could tell.

"This water is extra wet," she said. Rick laughed, patted her head as he walked past.

"Can I pee?" he asked, headed for the bowl. She didn't answer and kept her eyes focused on her long white legs, her underwater feet. Her toe girl was a fucking genius, the nails impeccably shaped and lacquered in high-gloss mauve.

Jill was embarrassed by the sound of Rick's stream, the easy intimacy of the act. Maybe he was finally starting to get high, too, and this was how he let her know.

"Your piss smells like popcorn," she said, and he laughed, spattering the toilet seat.

SOMETHING THUMPED FROM THE floor above them. A door slammed.

"People do other things in motels like this," she said. "Like dump torsos."

"That's what the reviews said. 'Fantastic for bloodless-torso dumping.'"

"Bloodless!" Jill said, delighted.

She jogged an arc around the foot of the bed.

"There was a place in my hometown like this," Rick said. "And they made a grisly discovery in one of the rooms."

"The best kind of discovery," Jill said.

"The guests complained about screaming, but when the authorities busted down the door—"

"Oh, God," Jill said, "here it comes."

"They busted down the door of the screamy room, and it was empty. But there's blood *soaked* into the mattress. It was, like, blood-sodden."

Jill was laughing now, losing it.

"And a body was never recovered, but due to the immense volume—"

"Immense!" Jill said.

"—authorities determined that the blood's owner, the body the blood belonged *inside* of, well, that person was most certainly dead."

"Oh, certainly," Jill said. "Most certainly."

"So that's my bloodless-torso story," Rick said.

"One of many, I hope," Jill said.

Then she said, "This dance is called the Skeleton." The last bump had pushed her a few clicks beyond sexy, which was actually a huge relief. She put her hands behind her back and clomped around, joints loose.

"What?" she said as Rick cracked up.

She stomped and jumped, let her head hang low. Rick wheezed, hysterical.

"Oh, fuck you," Jill said. "I'm a good dancer. It's because of the carpet. Plus, I don't have the right shoes."

Rick was quaking from where he was propped on the bed, his laugh a little ticking sound.

"WHAT ELSE SHOULD WE make me do?" Jill said.

"Do that thing where it looks like you're going down some stairs," Rick said, and Jill, her legs obscured by the edge of the bed, did it.

Rick clapped. He took a tube of lipstick out of her purse and twisted until the color came up.

"Here," he said. He grabbed her by the wrist and drew on her forearm.

"Wait," she said when he was finished, turning her arm so she could see. "Is that—what is that, a vulva?"

Rick snorted. "It's a kiss!" he said.

"You don't *draw* a kiss on somebody, idiot," she said. She swiped the tube across her lips. "You go like this," she said, and smacked a hot-pink print on the palm of his hand.

"Beautiful," he said, and waved at her.

"Tell me what else to do," Jill said, jogging in place.

"Okay," he said. "Do elevator."

"Elevator," Jill scoffed. "Here's better." She stretched, popped her neck. She looked straight ahead, gliding down on an invisible escalator. "Takes serious quads," she said. She did it again, this time whistling and looking at her watch.

"You get a big, fat prize," Rick said. He patted the pillow next to him. Jill flopped onto the bed on her stomach. They took turns with the baggie and the happy little key.

"Escalator reminds me. When I was a kid," Jill said, up on her elbows, feet slicing through the air behind her, "my mom would force me to go shopping with her."

"Forced!" Rick said. "My God! What an awful childhood."

Jill pressed her face into the bedspread. "We're gonna get diphtheria from this room," she said. "Just FYI." Rick said he hoped they got consumption instead.

"Being consumed," he said. "Yum."

"The mall was a problem, really," Jill said. She sniffed, touched her nose. "We were always ripping the tags off of stuff in the car before we went inside the house so my dad wouldn't freak out. And this is probably made up, but I even have a memory of my mom *eating* a receipt," Jill said. "Just popping it into her mouth and—" She mocked a sloppy chew.

Rick cackled. "No ketchup or anything?" He got up and headed for the bathroom.

"Come with me," he said. "Don't stop."

Jill trailed him. While he peed, she pressed her arms and legs out against the doorframe and tried to scale it. She talked to his back, noting with pleasure the hairy expanse at the base of his spine.

Jill said, "My mom even kept a laundry basket of dirty clothes in the trunk. She would bury the new stuff underneath, then smuggle the whole thing into the house. She bought things for me, too, to keep me quiet. Once she bought me a little crown, like Miss America."

"Whatever happened to the Miss Americas?" Rick asked. He finished but didn't flush.

"They're fine," Jill said. "Except for the very first ones. Those are definitely dead."

She stopped trying to hoist herself up in the doorframe. "Can I pee on your pee?" she asked.

Rick said, "But of course," and gestured grandly at the toilet.

"Look away," Jill commanded. She twirled a glove out of the toilet paper.

Rick splashed water on his face and looked in the mirror.

"It's a nice face," she said.

He said, "Thanks, I had them put the nose in the middle."

"Good choice," Jill said. "And I love the double eyes."

"You don't think it's too much?" Rick said.

"It got boring, buying shit, just another routine," Jill said. She peed slowly and pretended her piss was something else—glitter or confetti, falling beautiful and soundless. "I'd do things to entertain myself, hide in the racks of clothes, the usual stuff every kid does. But then I figured out how to walk *down* the *up* escalator very slowly, very casually. I was really good at it! My mom would stop shopping just to watch me. She'd be standing there, manic as fuck, shopping bags cutting off the circulation in her arms. We'd be criss-crossing the atrium at the mall, practically running from one store to the next, but at every escalator we passed she'd beg me to do it. We called it 'Stalled Time Machine,' and we both loved the shit out of it. I'd stand there on the escalator acting natural, just hovering, going nowhere.

"Okay, now *really* don't look," Jill said, and wiped.

Lined up along the sink were Rick's prescriptions in their amber bottles, a row of nothing good—blood thinners, cholesterol shit, statins—Jill had already checked.

"But your dad had to know, right?" Rick said, "I mean, presumably he *notices* your mom, like they live in the same house, he sees what she's got on. And one day he comes home from work and you're wearing a crown, right? Plus the money part."

"Oh yeah," Jill said. "He totally knew. And she knew he knew. I guess maybe it was all an act. Habit."

"Addiction theater!" Rick said.

"Fun for the whole family," Jill said.

They left the bathroom, and Rick lumbered up onto the bed. He rummaged around in the paper sack for more fries.

"Too bad there's no room service," he said.

"Oh my God, gross," Jill said. "Can you imagine?"

"You know who I wish was here?" Rick said, wistful.

"Sharkey?" Jill said.

"Yep," Rick said. "Sharkey."

"But he couldn't get the day off," Jill said, somber.

"He's got mouths to feed," Rick said.

"All those sharp little mouths," Jill said.

THEY'D PAID FOR THREE hours instead of the full day because they wanted to mark the passing time.

"We'll need a reason to leave the room," Rick said, "something to break things up." It was the best part of staying in a place like this.

He had gotten dressed, minus the tie, but she'd only pulled on her long camel coat over her bra and underwear. She belted it tight, stepped into her leather boots. Outside, two men in a parked car watched them stride into the tattered office. A woman flung a full gallon of milk into a garbage bin. Spoiled, Jill guessed.

Eyelash handled money matters in Rick's household. To avoid any suspicious charges Rick had been paying for things in cash, but now he'd run out, or said he had, so Jill needed to pitch in. Rick made more money than Jill did, of course, but not more than her husband. "Not even close," he reminded her. It was only fair that she should pay for some of the day's fun.

The guy behind the Plexiglas seemed to know what Jill

and Rick were up to, and Jill loved it, that feeling of being abhorrent, how it was expected, encouraged even, in a place like this. She touched her nose and slid her Amex through the open half circle.

"What are you going to tell Kneecap?" Rick asked her.

Her husband never looked at their credit card statements. Neither did she. "I'll tell him I went to the planetarium," she said. Rick howled. She laughed, too, and touched her nose again. The motel was called Starlite.

Jill signed her name, but something about her coiling script caused her to feel sick. She didn't usually day-drink, not since her chipped tooth, but she wanted a cocktail right then, to tone things down, and she asked the clerk if he sold spirits. On a rack behind him hung toiletries, little tubes of toothpaste, diapers, and lube.

"What, here?" the clerk said through his metal grate. "No."

"Seems like a missed opportunity," Jill said. "Business-wise." The clerk shrugged and said there were two liquor stores nearby. Jill asked which one he recommended. He shrugged again, not looking her in the eye. She loved this.

They walked to the closest place, and Jill waited while Rick went inside. He could pay for this, at least. Men were loitering, scratching lotto tickets, gripping brown bags and watching her. She looked them square in their faces, passed the time by stamping her long feet in her skinny boots, swishing her coat around. Rick came out and opened the paper sack for her. Inside was a bright yellow bottle—

a banana-flavored malt liquor called Monkey. Underneath was a package of Sweeties, pink cigarillos meant for celebrating the birth of a baby girl.

"Perfect," Jill said. "So good."

"There was a candy bar," Rick said, showing her a crinkled wrapper in his hand. "But it's over now."

HE'D HAD A LITTLE stroke the year before. "Just a blip," he said, but he'd missed months of work.

It had happened one night when he and Eyelash were sharing an extra-large pizza with everything. Earlier, Rick had finished some baggies alone in his Infiniti, in the parking garage at work. He was sitting in his easy chair, oily slice in hand, when the sight in one of his eyes switched off. The world strobed, and he heard all sorts of strange beats, a little rave right there in his skull. Later, the doctors said the pizza was as much to blame as the powder—it was a perfect storm of excess that constricted every vessel.

Jill passed a get-well card around the office and organized the flowers, a pot of ghastly birds-of-paradise she knew Rick would think was funny. She buried Sharkey lightly in the soil. Jill had no business visiting Rick in the hospital, so she watched him from afar. Various social media accounts showed a devoted Eyelash by Rick's bedside, spoon-feeding him, wiping his mouth. Jill kept everyone at the office updated—Rick's paralysis, his drooping face.

Jill worried that their friendship would falter, that the changes in Rick's life would exclude her. But he was fine now, more or less. His left hand wouldn't hold anymore. "It's okay," he said. "I've got this other one." He said he wasn't afraid of dying, that he'd gotten right next to death and it wasn't scary or sad. "It's like sitting after standing up for a long time," he said. He wasn't in any rush, of course, but at his age, he said, he was in slow drift, downward and forever.

When Jill asked if she could do anything for him, help him in any way, he told her he wanted two things. First, he wanted a pair of her panties after she had worn them for quite a while, to keep. Second, he made her promise she would never again ask if he needed help.

"That's not in your job description," he said.

THEY USED A STRAW from the orange soda to pull thick rails off the mirror he'd brought. It was a girls' hand mirror made of pink plastic, a unicorn stamped onto the back.

"What the shit is this?" she'd teased.

"What?" he said. "It's cute."

"It's *hers*," Jill said in mock outrage.

"It's not!" Rick said. "It's mine and it's lucky."

They'd been conservative before, and now they had quite a bit to get through. Jill looked at her phone.

"We've got time. We're up to the challenge," Rick said, tapping his thick finger at the full baggie.

They heard a thump above them and gave each other a look.

"What were you like in high school?" Jill asked.

"Exactly like this, minus the beard," Rick said.

He put his face close to the mirror.

"And everybody loved you," Jill said.

"Ha," Rick said. He came up and sniffed. "No. That was my older brother."

"I don't believe you," Jill said.

"He was the football player. Loved and feared."

"Yeah, but you're an adorable panda-person," Jill said. "And that must have been cool, right? To have a cool older brother?"

"He's the worst," Rick said. "When I was, I don't know, ten years old or something, he took me aside to teach me about women."

"Oh, boy," Jill said.

"He said, 'Ricky, when you see pussy, you gotta drill it.'"

"Holy shit," Jill said, and laughed. "Oh my God, that's the best advice."

"See, he would've charmed you," Rick said. "You sweet little minx."

"Oh, for sure," Jill said.

"He hasn't changed at all," Rick said. "He's in finance, drives a ridiculous car."

"Still drillin'?" Jill said.

"Real deep," Rick said.

There was another thump from upstairs.

"Bloodless," Jill whispered.

———

ON HER PHONE SHE could see her dog's four-legged avatar being walked in real time through the map of her neighborhood. The service was expensive, but the dog—a skittish cocker spaniel—was a rescue with intestinal issues. Jill flashed the screen at Rick, and they watched as little brown dots appeared: Muffin's shit.

"What?" Jill said. "It's cheaper than a new rug."

She told him then about the plant people, how she could track which flowers had been watered, how she got little alerts letting her know if her orchids were sickly. Rick howled at this, thought it was ridiculous, completely absurd, especially when Jill confessed what it cost.

"Oh, we have all the helpers," she said, but she didn't elaborate.

Rick made himself a little heart shape on the unicorn mirror and inhaled it.

"I don't want any more," Jill said, but he hadn't offered. She poured herself another Monkey, checked her watch, checked her phone. The fire escape map was in shadow, the slit of sunlight onto something new.

She was irritated. No matter how loud she turned up the music, she couldn't seem to hear the vocals. A walking bass line thrummed in her breastbone. Once, Rick had whacked the hood of a car for jutting into the crosswalk where he and Jill were passing, denting it like a monster with his huge hands. There was a black thread somewhere in him, Jill knew, but she couldn't seem to tease it out. Her husband had no such darkness.

"Tell me what you hate," she said. She stubbed out a Sweetie on the top of the dresser and lit another one. Her lungs were shrieking, but she wanted something to hold.

"I get annoyed when something is loose, like a water bottle or something, rolling around in the back seat of my car where I can't reach it," he said.

"Interesting," she said.

"You?" he said.

She minimized her hatred, matched it to his. "I hate the cotton that comes in vitamin bottles," she said flatly. "I don't know why."

He nodded in quick agreement.

She went to the mirror and reapplied her lipstick. Rick stayed propped up in bed, a crush of pillows under him, staring at her ass. She let her mouth gape like a corpse. She made a groaning sound over the throbbing music. Startled, Rick put his hand on his chest and laughed.

"Still gorgeous," he shouted.

She leaned into the mirror and groaned some more. Her pupils were nowhere. She looked deranged, her tongue a gruesome shade of yellow.

SHE HAD HER COAT off but her boots still on, her bra straps slipping down her shoulders. She'd been posing for pictures for him, letting him take them from behind or with her hands or hair covering her face. The music was soft, a track from a fuzzy fuck record she'd loved forever. Now she was on her side on the bed, an unlit Sweetie between her lips.

"Be still," he said.

He used his huge hand to pour powder onto the crest of her hip bone. He snorted, wiped the excess onto the revolting bedspread.

"Stupid," she said, and laughed.

"I've always wanted to do that to you," he said. "Your hips are like—"

"I know," she snapped. "They're good ones."

"MORE," JILL SAID. "BUT after this I'm done, even if I say I'm not."

She was straddling him, her bra off. She put her face in kissing range, but Rick didn't make a move. He was singing to her. Her hands were on his face, fingers laced in his big beard. He wasn't turned on—or his body wasn't, anyway—Jill could tell.

She glanced at her phone and saw that Muffin was no longer on the map. She wondered where he was curled up in her house, what he was doing right then. He was a beautiful dog, and one day, Jill thought, not long from now, he'd be dead.

Everything was not okay. She wanted Rick to kiss her so she could feel something else, and again she indicated this with her eyes, the position of her face. *Drill it, you fucking loser.* He kept singing to her, stroking her hair. She thought about her plants shriveling, her kind husband. Maybe it was the song that was ruining things—abysmal lyrics flitting over an easy melody, sweet as a TV jingle.

What did she expect? She recalled how once, on their lunch break at work, a strange girl sat down next to Rick on a park bench. Without saying a word, the girl took his arm, nuzzled against him, and fell asleep. Jill wouldn't have believed that story, but she had been there, on Rick's other arm, picking at a turkey sandwich.

She climbed off him and checked her watch, stared at her phone some more. At work, people would be starting to wrap up projects, thinking about the evening commute. Everything Jill's mind touched crumbled.

Rick studied her face, worried. He gently tugged one of her earlobes, but that was awful, something her husband liked to do. She felt a wave of nausea, but it wasn't Rick's fault. There were only so many body parts, so many ways to comfort. Aside from coming up with new, bizarre combinations—tapping someone's eyebrow, rhythmically stroking an armpit—there was no escaping the overlap. Rick put his hand on her thigh. She touched her nose.

"It's just the sads," she explained, sniffing. "It's not real."

Then she wasn't even sad anymore—just bored.

Upstairs, the thump returned, but soon Jill recognized it for what it was: a patter. Children were laughing above them, joyous, little feet in a filthy place. Nothing was dangerous.

The song ended and a different one started, synthetic swells, filtered voices. An arpeggiator climbed up and up a ladder of notes, and Jill felt the blood beating in her tongue. She imagined her head cracked open on a busy sidewalk, red rivulets streaming out beneath her hair. God, she loved this song.

Her hands were trembling, but she was fine now. "More?" Rick said.

ANOTHER SPIKE. RICK TOOK more pictures, but this time Jill left her face in full view. She wondered if he might one day put the images on the Internet, try to ruin her life. Maybe yes, maybe no.

Rick dumped the last of the baggie directly onto the dirty tabletop. "I'm the divider and you're the picker," he said. "Did you do this when you were a kid? To keep things fair?"

"I did," Jill said. "I totally remember doing that with my friends. Halloween candy, leftover birthday cake."

He carefully chopped the pile in half and she chose a side. The two of them dutifully took turns until the mounds were gone. Jill checked the time. Rick licked his finger and swiped through the dust.

"Tell me about you when you were a little boy," Jill said.

Right away Rick said, "I wanted to be a digger, you know?"

Jill didn't know.

"A digger?" he said. He made a scoop shape with his hand and moved it through the air. "Big yellow machine? I wanted to be one of those when I grew up," he said. "And I didn't, like, want to be the guy who operated the machine, a construction worker or whatever. I wanted to *be* the digger."

"Yes," Jill said, "yes! Keep going." She looked at herself

in the mirror behind Rick and switched the part in her hair, then switched it back again.

He was sweating, lit by the memory—even his dead hand was curled into a little bucket in his lap. "I would tell anybody who asked. And everyone did! 'Go ask Ricky what he wants to be when he grows up!' They thought it was so funny. My teachers, bigger kids. I had no idea why they laughed! I didn't care. A digger was what I wanted to be."

Jill nodded. "Yes," she said, "yes! I get you one hundred percent."

She scanned her life in preparation to tell a story, too, something funnier, even more adorable. There was the Stalled Time Machine thing! Ah, dammit. She would have to dip in deeper and find something precious, beat the fuck out of Rick's childhood. Rick's big pants were pooled on the floor and he was down on his knees, rifling through the pockets. Why wasn't he asking her about her life?

The song changed and it was the worst. Fucking minor chords.

Then Rick presented the surprise baggie, and Jill acted surprised and everything was good again. He poured out a fat heart just for her on the ridiculous mirror—this time with a slash shooting through it. Something pristine and wordless was swelling in her mouth. The space where her childhood should have been was a wad of gauze. She wished she knew little Ricky, all the wonderful Ricks in between, and the future Ricks, too—deathbed Rick, coffin Rick. Urn Rick, whatever. She checked her phone.

HE GOT UP TO piss again.

"If that's a horrible kidney stone you've got brewing inside," Jill said, "you'd better keep it for me."

"Of course," Rick said. "When the time is right, I'll pass it on to you."

"Pass it!" Jill said. "I'll have it polished and set. Princess cut."

When he came back he slid into the bed next to her. The song they called theirs came on.

"Aw," Rick said, pulling her into him. "You are so incredibly sweet."

"You knew it was coming," Jill said. "You had to know."

He touched her face. "I don't want to go back to normal," he said. But normal was always there, waiting.

Nothing about this day would keep. She imagined the two of them taking long lunches and constant smoke breaks, ducking in and out of the office like it was a bar. She imagined using Wite-Out to draw a big dick on the inside of Rick's desk drawer.

"Sometimes I can't tell which one of them is singing," Rick said. He reached over to the nightstand and grabbed a cupcake. "You know?"

"Do what?" she said.

"I mean, their voices are so similar, like they complement each other so well. I just can't always tell who is going up and who is going down."

Jill didn't say anything.

"What," Rick said. "Is that bad?"

"Is there any more?" Jill said. "In some secret pocket?"

"I wish," Rick said. He ate his cupcake and looked at the ceiling. "I really do."

"Do you?" Jill asked. Rick was a motherfucker. She thought about hissing at him, doing something so he'd see how crazy she really was. She was flat on her back, stark naked. She looked at her phone. Why *hadn't* her husband texted—was that unusual? She tried to remember a typical day in her real life. Maybe she should do a check-in? Just a "hey baby" to see how he was doing? Probably he was filing divorce papers at that very moment. She shivered and heard a high-pitched whine, like the ringing of a phone.

She whispered, "The call—it's coming from *inside* the ear."

"Huh?" Rick said.

Her nervous system was pissed off. "You should know which one is fucking singing, Rick," she said. "They're legends. This is, like, a timeless classic."

She thought about pinching him, hard. She spun through a quick, white-hot fantasy: he'd retaliate, they'd both leave this room with welts.

He put his head in her lap, gazed up at her lovingly.

"Forget it," she said.

"It's the mads," he said.

"I know, but also, I'm really, really mad," she said. She could already feel the rage falling away.

"You sure you're married?" he said. It was one of their jokes, meant to defuse her.

"I'm sure," she said. On more than one occasion, drunk bar strangers had approached Rick and demanded that he hug them.

"Is it serious?" he asked.

She sighed heavily, part of the bit. "I'm afraid it's terminal," she said.

EVENTUALLY HE CAVED, LIKE a good boy, and out came the secret-secret baggie. By then his nostrils were rebelling. He'd brought along a bottle of nose spray, and he spent some time at the edge of the bed, powering through his sinuses. She listened to the sound of his shifting mucus. She got up and did a series of obscene sun salutations. Rick watched. "Lift that scrim," he said.

The carpet by the window was a little bit damp, kind of spongy. Jill stood up and smelled her hands. She looked through the sheer yellowy drapes. People in the parking lot were walking in circles, their jaws moving.

She sat on the bed behind Rick and waited for him. She loved the shape of his head, his tiny ears. She used her phone to register a star in their names on the NASA website.

"I'm calling it Jick," she said. "We'll get an official certificate in the mail. Don't show it to Sharkey or he'll be jealous."

"The things you spend money on," Rick said, but Jill could tell he was touched.

After some time with the nose spray, Rick said, "Success!" and Jill brought him the straw.

"How many people have taken pictures of you like that?" he asked her, gesturing to the spot in the room where she'd been posing.

"So many," she said, and he cracked up at her quick answer.

Her heart was beating in her crotch. In her refrigerator at home was a head of purple cabbage, maybe a chicken breast. She could do the Thai thing Kneecap liked, something light. She put down her phone. She picked it up again.

"Do you want to know how much is left?" she asked. She thought it might be smarter to switch back to the key.

"Yes," he said, "but tell me in minutes."

He moved through a massive rail, then pulled her onto his lap, scooped her up like a baby. She pushed her face into his armpit and breathed.

JILL TUCKED HER TANGERINE silk blouse into her pencil skirt. She twisted her hair into a smart knot and secured it with a golden claw. She lipsticked, powdered.

Rick sat on the bed and watched her.

"You smell that?" he asked.

"It's my perfume," Jill said. She had spritzed her neck.

"No, not that," he said. He pointed upward with his wilted hand. "Food."

Jill tilted her head back and inhaled. Rick was right—

the scent of garlic and onions seeped through their ceiling, their neighbor's floor. Somebody was cooking dinner. Jill wondered if a hot plate was involved, maybe a portable stove. People lived here, of course. The last of the fun was fading, a weak pulse draining behind her eyes. The panicky feeling would stop once she left this room, got into her car and on the road. She had a song cued up for the drive home, ambient and unobtrusive.

She walked with alacrity, gathering what belonged to them. *This is how normal people move through the world,* she thought. She scooped up Rick's big pants, his tent of a shirt, and tossed them onto the bed.

"I'm getting my motivation up," he said.

"It's hard," she said, nodding. She was touching her face too much, reentering the atmosphere.

He had eaten both the burgers but offered her the rest of the cupcakes, said she should take them home to Kneecap. She politely refused. She punched her finger into a chocolate one, sucked at the frosting, then threw the whole box into the trash.

"Should we tip Housekeeping?" she asked, and they laughed. Jill imagined the desk clerk coming in after they'd gone, stomping their ashes into the moist carpet, fluffing the clammy pillows.

In the moldy bathroom she took Rick's pill bottles from the sink and shook them like maracas. She danced a solo conga back to the bedroom but then felt self-conscious and stopped. She lobbed the bottles at Rick in a slow underhand, but he didn't try to catch them—some landed in his lap and some bounced off his stomach and crashed on the carpet. Jill looked at her watch. Her boots were already on. She draped her camel coat over her arm. She'd have to have it cleaned. It had been on the floor, on the bed, stepped on, danced on. Maybe it couldn't be saved. She'd sat with her bare ass on it—both of them had used it as a tissue.

"Okay," she said. Rick was steeped in sweat, still propped up on the pillows. "It's time to go."

She'd get into her car and turn right, back past the office and down San Felipe to Piney Point, just like she did every day. She'd be home on time, maybe even early enough to take a shower before dinner. *Purple cabbage,* she thought. *Chicken breast.* Cooking would help. Measuring, seasoning. She dug through her purse. There was hand sanitizer in there somewhere.

"You know what?" Rick said. "Why don't you go ahead?"

"Huh?" she said. "I can wait." She touched her mouth, checked her phone. "We'd be walking out the door in, what, ten minutes?"

She put on her coat, belted it loosely. She had her sunglasses on her head, cat's-eye frames in oversize tortoiseshell.

"No, no, you should go," he said. He was breathing hard, but he was serene, stiff and permanent on the bed. Waiting for her to leave.

She cocked her head and looked at him.

"Seriously," he said. Then softer: "I'm a lazybones."

She had a flash then, complete and certain: big Rick on the gross bed, full baggies all around, the hours stretching out ahead. The room gritty and perfect, light getting dimmer and dimmer. Their phones so dead. Dancing and delicious streetlight, the zombies swinging their arms in the parking lot. Jill doing the splits naked on soggy carpet. Music throbbing from shitty, faraway car speakers, gunshots, maybe. Somebody pounding on the wall and them laughing. Singing the hits, the searing white sun. Posing like a cadaver. Slow yellow all day, then dim again, then dark, getting brighter. She'd paid such close attention— where had he hidden it? In his car, probably. She could confront him, and he'd confess everything, ask her to stay.

"Come on," she said. "Don't make your wife worry."

Jill had her purse on her shoulder, her body angled toward the door. She could get in her car and fall right back into her usual commute. Westheimer to Sage to San Felipe to Piney Point. Four easy turns. No, three.

"I work late sometimes," he said. "She knows that." He smiled at her, pulled at his beard.

She would shower instead of cooking, order Thai, and be clean, sitting on the couch in her white robe, reading a magazine when her husband walked through the door.

"Put your fucking clothes on," Jill said. She sniffed hard.

She could leave. She could. Inside the pocket of her coat, she held her house key in her hand, ready.

ACKNOWLEDGMENTS

THANK YOU TO MY BRILLIANT agent, Meredith Kaffel Simon-off—your unwavering support means everything. Margaux Weisman, you're a goddamn genius. You found the heart of the heart of these stories, and you showed me how to get there. Thank you to the teams at DeFiore & Company and Vintage: Jacey Mitziga, Tim O'Connell, Anna Kaufman, Angie Venezia, Kate Runde, and Mark Abrams.

Thank you to the literary journals that published versions of some of these stories: *The Best Small Fictions 2017, Black Warrior Review, Gigantic, Indiana Review, NANO Fiction, New South, No Tokens, Joyland,* and *Ninth Letter.* I am grateful for generous gifts from Columbia University, Writing by Writers, Hypatia-in-the-Woods, PLAYA, and the Sustainable Arts Foundation. Thank you to the Literary Studies Department at the University of Texas at Dallas, especially Dr. Robert Nelsen.

I owe so much to the Columbia faculty who helped shape early versions of these stories: Hilton Als, Rebecca Curtis, Jonathan Dee, Richard Ford, Sheila Kohler, Sam Lipsyte, Ben Marcus, Victoria Redel, and Alan Ziegler.

Thank you, Claire Vaye Watkins at the Tin House Summer Workshop, Rick Bass and Pam Uschuk at Elk River, and Lidia Yuknavitch at Writing by Writers.

Thank you, Alfred Brown IV, Emily Austin, Adam Boretz, Annie DeWitt, Patty Belsick, Dan Bjork, Genevieve Cole, Claire Comstock-Gay, Laura Hoffman, Jocelyn Johnson, Aram Kim, Belinda McKeon, Laura Stride, Molly Tolsky, Hannah Withers, Beth Feldman, and the amazing T Kira Madden.

Thank you, Gordon Lish, and thank you to the invaluable writing group that came after: Carrie Cooperider, Diana Marie Delgado, Mitchell S. Jackson, Joseph Riippi, Robb Todd, and Nicole Treska. Your eyes are the best first eyes.

Thank you, Dawn Raffel, for your editorial advice and early encouragement. Thank you, Tom Treanor and Wendy Flanagan, for your brilliant brains, our yearly trips, and all those beautiful meals. Eternal thanks to Melissa Duclos for making me hit Send.

Thank you, Melissa Bellaire, for being there all along. There's nobody I would rather have grown up with.

Mark Doten, beloved life-animal, thank you for every

damn thing, every step of the way. I could not have done this without you.

Chad Miller—violin smasher, best fake brother, the first feminist I ever met—thank you for teaching me how to read and whom to read and for treating me like a writer before I was one.

To my huge family—I love you (Daniel and Anna, we miss you so). Thank you to all six of my wonderful parents— the Kings, the Parsonses, the Ringos—for taking care of your grandsons so I could lock myself up and write. Special thanks to my dad for teaching me to appreciate music and to my mom for teaching me to appreciate the music of everyday conversation. I carry those lessons with me always.

Ronnie, I adore you—thank you is not enough, not even close. You model ambition and drive in your own brilliant work, and I'm so fortunate you understand what I'm trying to do with mine. Julian and Lev, you are the brightest lights, teaching me everything. You've made the world weird and wonderful and new again—I steal the best lines from your little mouths. How lucky that the three of you are mine, that I'm yours, that we get to spend this life together.